Visionary
A science fiction novel

Richard G. Hole

Science Fiction and Fantasy

SYNOPSIS

Two hundred years after the first atomic explosion in Hiroshima and Nagasaki, man had learned to use the force of the atom for something more useful and constructive than to annihilate himself.

In the year 2145 all the spaceships propelled by nuclear energy, capable of reaching the vertigo speeds of which he had always dreamed of.

However, the Universe continued to be infinite for him and the hypothetical surface of the planet Saturn unreachable ...

Visionary is a story belonging to the Science Fiction series, a collection of science fiction and fantasy novels

VISIONARY

CHAPTER I

Saturn now had eleven moons.

To its ten natural satellites, by the work and science of man, it had managed to place the artificial satellite in orbit, which was fulfilling its functions as a jealous observer of the planet adorned with the mysterious rings that surround it.

The "Saturn XI" was a small metallic world, a marvel of technology and electronics. At first glance, outwardly it was not much different from the other ten natural satellites, which since the long night of time had been revolving around the sixth planet in order from least to greatest distance from the Sun.

But inside, on the "Saturn XI" everything was different.

Five hundred human beings swarmed there, struggling to unravel the mysteries that enveloped the planet with the rings, to look to one day add to its long series of space conquests, man eager to dominate at least his entire solar system.

Behind, far behind, was the conquest of the Moon, that of Mars, Venus, Mercury and that of the giant planet Jupiter.

Observations and surveys of Uranus, Neptune and the distant Pluto, lost in the confines of the solar system, had also prospered, offering the inhabitants of the small Earth the limits that marked the outer hyperspace.

But now, before embarking on the fantastic adventure of going further in search of the stars, Saturn should remain under the intelligence of man, who seemed to be willing to never stop.

Never!

However, the difficulties were many. Since "Saturn XI", not only the data that had been known about the planet of the same name had been verified for a long time. That its equatorial diameter measured 119,700 kilometers, being, therefore, 9.4 times greater than that of the Earth, did not have much importance. As it did not have it, its volume was 745 times greater.

But the one who was at an average distance from the Sun of 1,430 million kilometers began to have it, since starting from its earth's crust, man had to travel with each thyme of his research instruments no less than 1,186 to 1,647 million kilometers , depending on the phase of your journey where you are.

Two hundred years after the first atomic explosion in Hiroshima and Nagasaki, man had learned to use the force of the atom for something more useful and constructive than to annihilate himself. In the year 2145 all the spaceships propelled by nuclear energy, capable of reaching the vertigo speeds of which he had always dreamed of.

However, the Universe remained infinite for him and the hypothetical surface of the planet Saturn unreachable.

Regarding its physical characteristics, it was known that its density was equal to 0.13 that of Earth and 0.72 that of water. It had been measured, ad nauseam, that the intensity of gravity on the surface of Saturn was equal to 1.06 compared to the gravity of the Earth, with an average light and heat received from the Sun of 0.011, taking as a unit the one received on the globe.

All this presented very difficult problems to solve, for making direct contact with the planet.

But there was more.

The surface of Saturn offers telescopic vision a whole series of bands or strips parallel to the equator, with a brownish-gray color, which stand out from the pinkish ones in the equatorial zone and the bluish ones in the polar regions. All this led us to suppose that Saturn was enveloped in a dense atmosphere and that it is only possible to observe the most extensive layer of it, whose temperature was being evaluated at about 150° below zero, as it was mainly made up of ammonia and methane.

The same white spots that could be seen from the artificial satellite "Saturn XI" were attributed to ammonia snow.

To make it more difficult, the planet was surrounded by a ring that appears as a meeting, a very complex grouping, of various concentric rings.

Regarding the real nature of this ring-shaped set of such striking appearance, its composition seems to be deduced by a huge number of astrolites isolated from each other, animated by a rapid turning movement around the central star and, approximately, in its same plane. The persistence and superposition of the images would give the feeling of continuity that was observed with the help of the most modern and powerful telescopes.

This natural barrier that the planet Saturn offered, as the first resistance to man's insatiable curiosity, was being studied in all its aspects.

If the concentric rings constituted a solid platform by the concentration of myriads of millions and millions of astrolites, the day would come when any spacecraft could land there: then the risky astronauts would be in an enviable position to take a look at the planet and, so to speak , to look inside that new world to finish, to conquer it.

All the scientists stationed on "Saturn XI" had accomplished much of their arduous task. They already knew that the dimensions of the set of rings were 278,000 kilometers in external diameter, with 149,000 in internal diameter. That they had a width altogether of 67,400 kilometers; a thickness of 70 kilometers and an annular mass with respect to the planet of 1/600.

And all this in less than a year of being there, turning and turning like one more satellite of Saturn, 1,647 million kilometers from Mother Earth, which had sent them as forecasters of the progress of their supercivilization that refused to admit barriers.

Aside from examining Saturn's rings, the task focused on the immediate possibility of being able to land on all of its ten natural satellites.

Ideal platforms placed there by the mysterious gravitational law of the Universe, it was intended with their conquest the great saving of other orbital stations that were needed.

This was not an unrealizable dream, considering that there were already astrophysical observatories on the surface of the Moon. The question was to descend in one of the ten natural satellites of Saturn, study it, overcome the difficulties that it presented and settle there.

In order from least to greatest distance from the planet, "Mines" and "Enceladus" were 185 and 238 thousand kilometers away, respectively. «Tetis», «Dione» and «Eea», at 294,337 and 527 thousand kilometers, also respectively. "Titan" was turning at 1,223 thousand kilometers, "Temis" at 1,460, "Hyperion" at 1,484, "Yapeto" at 3,563 and "Fepe" at 12,950 thousand kilometers.

A faithful and numerous family, to which a new son of science had joined: the "Saturn XI", which rotated at sixty million kilometers presiding over that eternal dance of celestial bodies around the planet to be conquered.

But the most important of these moons was "Titan", having a diameter of 4,200 kilometers and a mass equivalent to 1.8 greater than that of the Moon. It was one of

the few satellites of the planetary system that present an atmosphere, although the measurements carried out in the laboratories of "Saturn XI" indicated that such an atmosphere could be highly harmful to humans, as it contains acids and forms of poisonous salts.

Of course, this would not be exactly what would stop him.

On the surface of Mars it was not possible to breathe freely either and yet, creating the necessary means, already lived there a terrestrial colony of more than two hundred million people.

Or was it that a mad poet had not sung, that man would put his sinful feet on the same red-hot surface of the father sun ...?

And, in a way, crazy poets are the fortune tellers of the future.

Or not...?

CHAPTER II

Jerry Kelly was one of these crazy poets.

Although he did not compose poetry or waste his time in the composition of more or less rhythmic and successful odes.

Young Jerry Kelly's "madness" was science. Specifically acoustic science, determined for many years to give concrete form to some daring theories of his father that, unfortunately when he died, he had not been able to finish.

But Marty W. Kelly had left his son enough data for Jerry to continue his work. Above all, he had left him the conclusion of his daring theories in all matters concerning sound, the vibrational waves moving incessantly in space and a great accumulation of data on his immutable laws, thehertz and all those complicated names that complete the science of acoustics.

What the wise Marty W. Kelly had not left when he died was fortune, and therefore the necessary means for his son Jerry to continue the study of such expensive investigations.

Due to this, Jerry Kelly had not been able to carry out his experiments in a satisfactory way, and at the same time he was forced to accept one of the positions among the prominent ones on that artificial satellite, placed in orbit around Saturn.

And on "Saturn XI", more than a billion kilometers from Earth, isolated in that small metallic world where 499 other people also worked, in their spare time, once they had fulfilled their duties as an electronic engineer specialized in sound, he struggled to make his invention.

An invention of which he used to say with emotion:

"It will revolutionize our entire civilization, making it more noble, more pure ... Much more human!

But very few did he speak about what "his invention" really would be.

Jerry Kelly remembered doing it in the early years of his experiments, even though his father's death was recent, with the unpleasant result of having been mocked. And not only the individuals who did not understand all those things he was talking about, but also the most prestigious research centers, who ended up telling him, after listening to his strange theories:

"Keep investigating, young man. And when you obtain a positive result, do not doubt that we will put at your disposal the necessary means to make your dream come true.

Nice way to excuse that one!

How could he continue investigating on his own, if precisely what he lacked was that, the means?

Jerry Kelly had calculated that he needed a well-equipped laboratory, with the latest advancements and the ability to create the machines and delicate instruments that he needed. Unfortunately, it was not a question of "inventing" a single device, however sensitive and complicated it might be, but of many, many others that were completed as a whole.

To begin with, he needed a spacecraft capable of traveling through space at breakneck speeds, sinking into the bottomless blackness of hyperspace to pick up the waves of the sounds he sought. That alone was already an obstacle that he could never overcome on his own.

How could a private individual own one of those modern spacecraft that made interplanetary travel?

Then came the ultrasensitive antenna system, the complex set of tape recorders, the delicate mechanism that should bring into play the way of filtering and separating sounds; the recording tapes of those same sounds, the sorting station and ...

It was exasperating!

And yet Jerry Kelly never lost faith that his wonderful invention would one day be a reality.

A reality that, as he firmly claimed, would completely transform society.

Words ... Words ... Words!

Yes: it was precisely on Jerry Kelly's "words" that he based his theories. In the billions and billions of words that the human being had been releasing throughout his passage on the face of the Earth, from the same day in which for the first time he stammered something intelligible, when trying to understand himself with others.

From the moment that the human being stopped being a beast, emerging from barbarism, to gradually become, in the eternal night of the centuries, a rational being.

In a higher creature.

So superior that at more than one time in his long history, full of pride, he had been on the verge of challenging his own Creator, using barbarous destructive methods to annihilate himself.

As happened when he discovered the use of gunpowder.

As happened when he managed to use dynamite, trilite, the terrible nitroglycerin.

Like when he was about to be exterminated, when he managed to disintegrate the chain reactions of the fearsome atom.

None of these critical stages in the history of man could be repeated, if one day the dreamer Jerry Kelly managed to make his invention available to Humanity.

Although at the moment he couldn't offer anything more than that either.

Words.

Words in the form of promises, which had always had little echo.

Little echo until he spoke with the astrophysicist Walter Lehman, responsible for the operation of "Saturn XI" and in charge of those half a thousand men and women assigned to the orbital station.

A few days after reaching his destination, Jerry Kelly told him about the reasons for his request, announcing the elderly scientist:

"Here, as long as you know how to fulfill your obligations, you can use your free time in whatever you want.

Thank you Professor Lehman. I applied for this position because the "Saturn XI" can be an excellent platform for my experiments.

"Has that possibility alone brought you here, Kelly?

Jerry Kelly had reflected, before answering, quite frankly:

"Just that, professor.

"Are you not scientifically curious about Saturn?

"None, sir. I'm only motivated by acoustics

Astrophysicist Walter Lehman had reflected in his turn, running his well-fingered hand through his frizzy gray hair, in a usual movement for him to comb it. And it was when he wanted to know, always driven by his scientific desire:

"Tell me about your theories about sound, young man. You are beginning to interest me!

Indeed, Jerry Kelly found his theories quite confusing and complicated for a layman. But before him he had an eminent man, recognized as wise in astrophysics, space aeronautics and with a privileged brain, and for that reason he tried to explain:

"You see, Professor Lehman ... You know that, although both the mechanical medium that causes it and its appreciation by the ear, physically considered, is accepted as 'sound', it is a vibratory movement originating in a body, which is transmitted to through elastic material means and that, when brought to our ear, produces the physiological sensation of sound.

"I understand, young man. As a vibrating object enters, it sets the surrounding air in motion, thus creating pressure zones that you specialists call "sound waves."

"Exactly, professor! "Exclaimed his young subordinate enthusiastically." I see your clear understanding with real joy, sir.

"Continue please.

"The 'sound waves' propagate in the air in a way similar to that of the series of concentric rings that form on the surface of a pool of still water, when a stone is thrown into it.

"True: that can be verified by anyone.

"That's right, sir. But if anyone can see it in the water, not in the air, because you can't see those "sound waves."

The silence of the manager of the "Saturn XI" encouraged young Jerry to continue:

"Nor is it given to anyone to verify, for example, that if that stone is thrown into the ocean, the concentric waves will reach, saving all the difficulties they encounter in their expansion, to the most secluded shore, and once they have reached the shore opposite, however distant it may be, they will return in an endless movement that, no less perceptible and more and more muffled, is less real.

"And from what it says, the same thing happens in air, in space, when a sound is produced, right?

"Exactly the same, Professor Lehman! Exactly!

"Very interesting to remember that!

"Sound waves are also spherical, they always propagate at the same rate or frequency, according to the vibration that originated them. Except in those cases in which the sound-producing organ is in motion, losing only in amplitude or intensity in relation to the square of the distance.

The hand of the old astrophysicist invited with kind rest, after stopping combing his hair, adding his young interlocutor:

"All elastic materials, like most metals, wood, air, water, transmit sound waves at speeds generally higher than that of the atmosphere. Specifically, in air, the velocity of propagation is 331.8 meters per second, at a temperature of 0 ° C, increasing by approximately 0.60 per degree of increase.

Walter Lehman smiled at the last thing, aware that he was not, however wise, as aware of the data as the acoustic engineer Jerry Kelly. But following his idea, he inquired:

"And don't weather conditions, wind speed, ambient humidity and atmospheric pressure influence the propagation of sound, for example?

"Of course Mr. But all these are data to take into account in the specialization, when we want to "recover" a sound that we know has been released in such a place, at that time and in such or such circumstances.

Professor Walter Lehman's scientific curiosity was sharpened, forcing him to ask, increasingly interested:

"Just a moment! Does it imply that any sound that has been thrown into the ether can be "recovered"?

"That's right, sir.

"Any sound that caused sound waves?

"Yes, Professor Lehman.

"For example ... the vibrations that our voices produce when we speak now? Could you grasp them, "get them back," as you just said?

"Yes, Mr. Lehman. And that's what I try!

"When could I get them back?

"When I have all my instruments, it will be the same to capture them, or rather, « recover » them, within an hour ... or a century!

"Do not!

"Excuse me for insisting, professor. And not a century from now, but ten thousand years from now, if we have the necessary means to do so.

"Please, Kelly... will you explain it to me?

"With pleasure, professor. Note that in this case we have the most accurate data. First, the sound produced by the vibrations converted into "sound waves" of our words, which we know at the speed at which they travel in their normal environment. Second, the place and the exact time that those words were launched into the air, or into space, if you want to say so. Then, with launching ourselves in their search with an ultramodern tape recorder equipped with an oscilloscope also ultrasensitive, the problem would be to explore the area where we calculate "mathematically", by electronic brains, which "are" scattering in increasingly enlarged concentric circles those words that we wish to "recover", said in this room ...

"What you say is amazing, friend Kelly!

"It is, Mr. Lehman. But basically simple, and eternal, like all the immutable laws that govern the Universe.

"And those... those sounds that our words make, can't they come out of this room, this space station, the« Saturn XI »? I mean if they don't come out to be lost forever.

"They can go out, professor. Lost forever, no.

"Sure?

"If man has the technical means to go after these 'sound waves', somewhere he will 'hunt' them, so to speak.

"I repeat, my young friend ... That is very interesting!

"Until now, Professor Lehman, man has let out all those sounds, losing that immense wealth in space.

Somewhat surprised by the qualifier, the astrophysicist in charge of "Saturn XI" repeated like an echo:

"Wealth says?

"I consider enormous wealth to be the words they spoke, for example ... Pythagoras, Socrates, Plato, Aristotle, Jesus Christ ...

He paused, before adding, vividly:

"Anyway ... Everything, sir! Everything that has been spoken and said, since man had the power to speak!

"But that... that would be wonderful, my young friend! Do you know what he said?

"Perfectly, Professor Lehman. Something that I have been repeating here and there in various places ... But without getting them to listen to me seriously!

Walter Lehman smiled kindly as he calculated, again combing his tousled gray hair as he said:

"Now I understand that in many places they have taken him for a madman.

"Believe me, sir. It has been exasperating!

"I'm honest with you, Kelly. It is also hard for me to admit that what he says may one day become a reality!

"Well, we have it at our fingertips, professor. I've been working on it for many years! And previously my father did it for more than half his life.

"The truth, Kelly ... I think your enthusiasm makes you believe that it will soon be achieved.

"Not my enthusiasm, sir! Do we not already have spaceships that cross the outer spaces, sinking at dizzying speeds in the infinite black of the Universe? What prevents us from equipping them with ultra-sensitive oscilloscope antennas designed by me, capable of capturing all the sounds that "travel" in the sound waves, bouncing here and there, or always spreading and spreading in concentric circles, as when we have given the example of the stone thrown into the pond?

"Let's admit that, Kelly. But they would pick up all the sounds. All the noises!

"Without a doubt, professor. But today it is child's play to "select" the sounds. Recording and reproducing sounds is a very advanced science, ever since Edison invented his phonograph. Since then, many years have passed and today we have magnificent recorders. In addition to that, properly selected and arranged filters would discard all sounds that were not the human voice, with well-arranged amplifiers to restore all its nuances, all the inflections of the speaker. Hertz ...

"The what, Kelly? "Inquired the elderly astrophysicist." I see that, carried away by his enthusiasm, he forgets the simplicity in his explanation, without realizing that I am not a specialist in the matter.

"Excuse me, sir" Jerry Kelly acknowledged. A "hertz" is the unit of frequency equivalent to one vibrated or cycle per second. The frequency range audible to the human ear ranges from 16 Hz to 30,000 cycles per second. Today we know that the ear does not have the same hearing capacity for all frequencies, its sensitivity being greater in the range between 400 to 3,500 cycles per second.

Walter Lehman smiled again, thinking aloud:

"And do you think we could hear the great Carusso sing, of whom the story of the opera tells us; to a Renata Tebaldi or to anyone else who, for example, would have sung at the Scala in Milan or at the Metropolitano in New York?

"Why not? "Exclaimed, full of absolute certainty, his interlocutor." And even with all the primitive richness of its nuances, its intonations and its beautiful voices.

"Do not tell me!

"Well, it will be like that! For this we will only have to know exactly the place, the exact time in which it acted, know as much as possible, if it is possible, the weather conditions of that day or that night, group, qualify and select other important data, submit them to the previous review from a specialized electronic brain or a computer, to then go on to capture, to "rescue" with the powerful ultrasensitive and oscilloscopic antennas that I told you, those voices that continue to spread through space infinitely. Then the task of selecting them will come from among the many other noises that are captured and ... that's it!

"So easy, my dear Kelly?

"It's that easy, once all the complicated instruments for which I have been sighing for so many years are obtained.

"There is no doubt, young man. If you get that ... it will be amazing!

"It is, it is enough to imagine what it would mean to possess in infinity of tape recorders, perfectly selected by periods, subjects, disciplines and events, not only everything that the wisest men who have existed in past generations have spoken, but each one and all the words of the human race, since what we call civilization exists. This "library" would be like living books, the textbooks of the future, putting at our fingertips the most accurate thoughts, the highest feelings, the most intimate secrets.

The elderly Walter Lehman could not help but gape when he heard that exalted young man continue to expound with heat:

Hearing the voice of a Socrates when he spoke with his beloved disciples. Listen to the wise and resigned advice of a Seneca addressed to Nero. Hearing from the lips of a Goethe his own poems. Feeling that the voice of William Shakespeare recites his immortal works. Listening to the monologues that a great writer like Dostoevsky must have given during his sleepless nights or listening to a Beethoven play the piano, must be such an immense pleasure as well as so educational, that any means to make it possible is insignificant, no matter how much. it may cost.

Cocking his gray head in pleasure, Walter Lehman muttered:

"Yes ... It must be delicious!

"But there is more, professor! And not because of what philosophers, thinkers, writers, musicians, poets and other people of great value can give us with their own voices. It will be wonderfully definitive because in the face of all these first-hand testimonies, many misunderstandings, many bad intentions, many historical errors and many false interpretations, intentional or not, would be clarified. Many lies will cease to be, many falsehoods now covered up will come to light, and with it truth and justice will shine as they have never shone since the world is world.

"I'm afraid that would not please many, Kelly,

"To hell with the friends of the tapujos, the entanglements and the lies, sir! To hell with all hypocrisy or error!

"I am thinking that the conversations of not a few rulers, nowadays held by irreproachable people, would also come to light. Well, there are not a few conspiracies sustained with the greatest secret, which we do not know!

"So what, professor? I have for me that who likes to live in error and perpetuating deception and lies is not very worthy.

"True, young man, true ... But do you calculate the one that could be rolled?

"There each one with his conscience, sir!

With the wings of his imagination, the wise scientist must have seen all a tremendous chaos that made him exclaim, although half amused:

"Good God what would happen, my son!

"I calculate it, theday when powerful squadrons of spaceships would sail through space capturing with their antennas and ultrasensitive devices the words that would be selected from all the other noises. Once the ships returned to the laboratories and that selection was further nuanced, it would be possible to know, for example, what the last mechanic of the "Saturn XI" is saying to his close friend right now.

"That awful! That would be violating a right that ...

"A misunderstood right, professor. We are used to respecting things that at the same time allow the most evil to carry out their plans. Every good man usually has nothing to hide.

Jerry Kelly paused before adding, to partly reassure the man who could help him:

"Besides, Professor Lehman ... When my invention is made, if we do not want to create chaos and destroy many reputations by coming into possession of dark secrets, we will have to be very careful. I estimate that only top management positions will be able to access these confidential recordings.

"It is seen that all inventions have their faces and their cross, my young friend. And I guess if yours can bring enormous satisfaction, it can also bring enormous problems.

"But progress should never be denied, Mr. Lehman. At the end of the day, everything that brings us closer to the knowledge of the truth is moral and, therefore, recommended, sir.

"I'm afraid the absolute truth still scares us.

"Time will come when it will not be like that.

"Do you think it can be used for people's self-education?

"Why not? When they are certain that everything they speak or say, even in the greatest secrecy, can be "recovered", they will inevitably become less intriguing, less liars ... More pure!

"You apparently dream of an ideal world, young man.

"Is it a sin to do so, professor?

"No, it is not a sin. But a wonderful madness!

"I have heard that word many times. My poor father was also rated that way on many occasions. But I know I'm not crazy, sir! I'm not!

"I'm not saying such a thing, Kelly.

"You see ... It will be a matter of an ascending process: we will start by measuring the words, from which the facts and actions are normally derived. The behavior of all mankind will gradually change. Until the day that any of the men or women show themselves to others as they originally were.

"What was said! You are a wonderful madman!

"Then, you will only have your thoughts left, although the day will come that these too will be exposed to the clear light.

Walter Lehman got up behind his monumental desk as if to indicate that the interview was over, but not without smilingly commenting:

"It was a real pleasure listening to you, Kelly. And in advance, I promise to do everything in my power to keep you working on your project.

"I really appreciate it, professor.

"Moreover, if you allow me, in my spare time I will collaborate with you, and I have no problem in becoming your assistant.

"Oh no sir! Professor Walter Lehman could never be a simple assistant of mine. You are well known for ...

"But not understanding anything about your specialty, Jerry! And believe me, I am passionate about your idea.

"If it really is so, I am pleased to have left everything on Earth and to be here now.

"Have you left a lot, Jerry? The old man wanted to know.

Jerry Kelly was silent before answering:

"Everything I had, professor.

"A woman, maybe ...?

"Yes ... We were going to get married, but she never fully understood me. On the other hand, when I sometimes started talking to him about all that, too ... he also called me crazy or visionary!

Smiling to remove solemnity from his words, the elderly astrophysicist commented:

"In that case, you have come to fruition. Here we are all crazy! Don't you. Does it seem crazy enough to request to live more than 1,600 million kilometers from our beloved planet?

"Perhaps, sir. But, as you said before, it is a marvelous madness because thanks to the fact that there have always been such "madmen", Humanity has been able to progress.

"We agree, young man.

And the two men shook hands with great emotion.

At last, Jerry Kelly had found someone who completely understood him.

CHAPTER III

A month and a half after his first interview with the man responsible for the operation of the "Saturn XI," Jerry Kelly was able to present results and was therefore satisfied.

On the tenth floor of the artificial satellite, next to the hangars where the five spacecraft that the "Saturn XI" was equipped with were lined up, the elderly astrophysicist Walter Lehman had allowed him to set up his laboratories.

A series of interconnecting rooms, lined up on the top floor so that their ceilings could be partly open to the outside, contained the delicate ultra-sensitive instruments that Jerry Kelly had been assembling with the help of his collaborators.

People like him, destined for the "Saturn XI", but who did not hesitate to use their free hours on this new project. Jerry had told them about his theories in Acoustics and the old dreams that his father could not realize.

After much discussion and agreement, this fantastic project was christened "The Voice of the Universe."

Jerry Kelly had accepted the suggestion of his fellow collaborators, in reasoning with them:

"I like that" Voice of the Universe "thing! Because, indeed, it will be the Universe that will "speak" to us. We, with the help of these instruments that we are building, will capture all the sounds that travel in space. And the stars will trust us with their secrets!

Most of those who voluntarily joined the task did not understand a word of Acoustics. But they were young, they were also enthusiastic about science, and with lively words, with his characteristic vehemence and warmth, Jerry knew how to explain what his "invention" would be and everything that could be achieved with it.

On the other hand, if your collaborators were not specialists in sound issues, they were in other subjects. For example, Billy Laughton and the blonde Ramy Piccole were electronics engineers. Michel Sauet was an expert in mechanical matters, capable of designing, assembling and building the most complicated mechanism, as long as he was given a full idea of what was required of him. The Herculean Arthur Hadmond was a genius in electrodynamics, and the beautiful woman Marlene Power had not long been a doctorate in Cybernetics, that complicated science that takes care of the art of building and operating devices and machines that, by means of electronic procedures, they carry out automatically complicated calculations and other similar operations.

With this effective help and, above all, with the determined support of the elderly astrophysicist Walter Lehman, who ruled that small colony of five hundred outstanding human beings in space, Jerry Kelly hoped very soon to achieve his goal.

"The voice of the Universe" would soon be heard.

They only needed to equip with the same instruments, but reduced to a smaller size, to any of the five spaceships they had. Then they would carry out the necessary calculations with the help of the electronic brains that they had already assembled, so that the ship would go out to "recover" the words that, always according to Jerry Kelly's theories, continued incessantly through the centuries stretching out into infinite space. .

Jerry Kelly would have liked to choose a defining moment in the long history of man. For example, he had dreamed of "recovering" the words of Jesus Christ when he spoke to his disciples the afternoon he delivered his wonderful "Sermon on the Mount."

But hearing directly nothing less than the word of the Son of God was still a dream dream. And not because it was so many centuries ago; that was a simple matter of computer calculation. The electronic brains would take care of the necessary equations, taking into account all the data that was supplied to them.

So many centuries, so many years. So many months, so many weeks. So many days, so many hours, minutes, seconds and hundredths of a second.

"Total, nothing" said Jerry.

It would also be easy to calculate where the sound waves that entered into vibration when the divine words were pronounced would be spreading. The Universe was immense and, therefore, according to the laws of Acoustics, they would be somewhere in space, spreading more and more.

Jerry Kelly was a brilliant specialist on all of these issues. He knew by heart the distance sound traveled in one second: under normal circumstances and at a temperature of $0\,^{\circ}C$, at 331.8 meters, increasing by approximately 0.60 per degree.

"I tell you" he insisted. Matter of calculation!

If in one second the sound traveled 331.8 meters, in one minute it would manage to bridge the distance of 19,908; in one hour, 1,194,480; in a day, 28,667,520, and in a year, 10,463,644,800 meters.

Ten thousand four hundred sixty-three million and six hundred sixty-four thousand eight hundred meters divided by one thousand left ten million four hundred sixty-three thousand six hundred forty-four kilometers, with a remainder of eight hundred meters. There was nothing more than to multiply this amount by a hundred, to find out how many kilometers the sound traveled in a century. If history said that Jesus Christ lived in Galilee twenty-one and a half centuries ago, more or less, there was nothing more to do another arithmetic operation.

Total: with these calculations not made to the second or rigorously, the words that the Son of God threw to the wind would continue to spread to a distance from the Earth of the order of twenty-two billion kilometers from their starting point.

But they themselves, constantly circling the planet Saturn, were they not already about two billion kilometers from Earth?

With its ultrasensitive antennas attached, the spacecraft would have nothing more to go twenty billion kilometers to "hunt down" the desired sound waves.

And did not the astrophysicists and the most eminent men of science ensure that, once outside the Solar System, already gliding through outer hyperspace, free from the gravitational force of the System, the spaceships could see their speed a hundredfold?

What, then, was that distance to be bridged?

"It is going towards infinity! "Said Dr. Marlene Power, one of the days when they discussed those problems.

With his dreamy eyes, Jerry Kelly stared at the young scientist and thought seriously:

"This is precisely what must have always been the way of man, my dear friend. Infinity!

In any case, Jerry Kelly had to do without capturing with his ingenious acoustic mechanisms those divine words that he so longed for and would have liked to be able to offer to the world. History did not give the necessary precise data on the life of the Son of God; at least, as regards the time and place where he was preaching his divine doctrine at any given moment.

"How about the speech that President Abraham Lincoln gave after the Battle of Gettysburg? Proposed electronic engineer Billy Laughton.

"Yes, Jerry! "Clinched his partner Michel Sauet." We do have accurate data on those dates. Exact place, fixed date and everything else.

"Studying history, I read that speech by President Lincoln" recalled the blonde Marlene Power, joining them. It is wonderful!

"It will be more so when you can hear it himself" assured Jerry Kelly, apparently accepting the proposal of his companions.

"Do you really think you can do it, Jerry? "The girl wanted to confirm.

"You said wrong, Marlene. We all work here as a team! Therefore, to achieve it, it will be a triumph for all. .

"Protest! Shouted the gigantic and Herculean Arthur Hadmond, with his loud voice of thunder.

They all looked at him, leaving work, gathering around the senior electrodynamicist, who added, trying to restrain his tone:

"Yes friends. I said I protest!

"Why, Arthur?

"Because we are nothing more than simple acoustics learners. Here; Jerry is the one in charge, and we only help him to assemble the devices he indicates.

Jerry Kelly looked at the big man gratefully, but saying:

"You are very kind, Arthur, but I insist that I do not seek personal glory in this. Rather, it is like ... Yes, friends: like "something" that I have been inside for years and I am eager to let go, so that I can offer it to all of humanity.

He cocked his head as he always did when reflecting or remembering something, adding, after a brief pause:

"I remember when my father was already working on this. I was very young at the time and could not fully understand everything he was teaching me. Those complicated equations and all those calculations bored me!

"Your father was one of the twelve wise men at the Wilder Institute. Right, Jerry? Marlene Power wanted to know.

"Yes ... He won some very close competitive examinations and they gave him the chair of Acoustics, but ...

With his usual brusqueness, always marching straight into things, Arthur Hadmond tried to guess:

"Died...?

"Yes, Arthur... By accident. One afternoon something exploded in his laboratory and he was found charred. Fortunately, all the designs and plans were at home. I lived with an aunt of mine who ...

The visophone began to buzz and the screen lit up, showing Professor Walter Lehman's wrinkled face. The communication came directly from the office of the director of the "Saturn XI" and he announced, in his loud excited voice:

"Is Jerry around?

Jerry Kelly approached the apparatus, aware that the screen would reflect his image in the astrophysicist's office.

"You will say, professor.

"Hi, Jerry. Will you please come? I have to notify you of something.

The buzzing stopped when the screen was switched off.

They all approached the young acoustics engineer, but it was the blonde girl who spoke:

"What's up, Jerry?

"I don't know, Marlene. But I thought I noticed some dryness in the professor's voice.

"I have also noticed it", put in Michel. He spoke as when he is worried about something.

Jerry Kelly reached out for his volunteer volunteers and announced:

"Okay for today, folks. How about we meet again in the dining room?

"I would like to finish that dynamo that gives me so much war and ...

"You know I have to close these rooms, Billy. The security system requires it.

"Okay, I'll do it tomorrow.

They all went out and Jerry Kelly manipulated the board next to the door so that the photoelectric cells registered the password that only repeating it would allow someone to enter those metal rooms, hermetically sealed by the remote control.

Through the moving corridor, they reached the elevator, which was distributed to the other floors, each having to return to occupy their position on the space station.

The last to say goodbye was Marlene Power, who announced, before Jerry Kelly walked into the director's office of the "Saturn XI":

"Don't miss dinner, Jerry ... I want to ask you about those damn antennas.

"You still haven't solved the problem, Marlene?

"No... It's harder than it sounds. If they must have the wavelength that you request, in the oscilloscopes we will have to put more cells of magnetized isotopes with the specific weight of ...

The blonde girl stopped, smiling as she said goodbye:

"Don't keep the boss waiting now, Jerry. We will talk later.

"You are right. Until later, Marlene.

Minutes later, the doors of the monumental office of the director of the "Saturn XI" were opening.

And Jerry Kelly saw in the face of the elderly Walter Lehman that, indeed, something very serious must be going on.

CHAPTER IV

The first word that sounded in that room was this:

"It's over!

Jerry Kelly walked over to the table behind which the old professor was sitting. He thought that he had misheard and inquired, without daring to sit down as before:

"How did you say, Mr. Lehman?

"I said it's over, Jerry. No more acoustic experiments!

"But, sir ... Now that we've worked so hard, when we're about to get it and ...

"You know better than anyone the interest I have put into this, boy. You know it very well!

"That is precisely why, Mr. Lehman. I don't understand how now ...

Walter Lehman stopped combing his gray hair with his fingers, before lowering his hand to a piece of paper on the table and offering:

"Read this, Jerry. Maybe I'll clarify it ...

Jerry Kelly quickly read the statement. It was a radiated message, coming from the mother spacecraft, the one that made the trips from artificial satellite to satellite, supplying what it in turn was receiving from distant Earth.

In short, that statement warned: No more acoustic experiments on the "Saturn XI." All work carried out outside the programmed study of the planet and the constitution of its rings will be considered a fraud. And for the useless waste of the valuable material that is used, the director of the "Saturn XI" will be responsible.

Jerry Kelly looked at the elderly astrophysicist and muttered, increasingly concerned:

"Do you think: do you think this will harm you, sir?

Walter Lehman gave a slight shrug as he muttered:

"It's obvious, Jerry. In the assembly of your laboratories we have used very valuable material. Machines and instruments built here, which they ... They do not approve!

"They, sir?

"Clearer, Jerry. The Governing Board of the Saturn Program.

"Who presides over it?

"Peter Masson, a man who until now was a good friend and who did not object when, in the first communications, I brought him up to date. Of course, he told me that as long as that work did not interrupt the program, in your hours of rest you could do whatever you wanted. Later... .

Jerry Kelly did not interrupt that pause, listening to him add:

"Last week I asked for the filter plates that you asked for. Apparently the mothership did not have this delicate material and in turn requested it from Earth. You know that they see things more meticulously there and that the entire Saturn Program must be approved by the Wilder Institute. Good...

New pause before finishing:

"Apparently, when Charles Wilder found out, he screamed. At this time, an investigating Commission for the case is coming here. I have lost my position!

Walter Lehman was already many years old, but at that moment he still seemed much older. It was no secret to anyone that this man had been in space for more than half his life. A pioneer in the conquest of Mars, he had later taken part in the first direct contact with Venus, Mercury and Jupiter. It was precisely on the giant planet that he had obtained the precious "Einstein" award, for a certain revolutionary system that made it possible to provide the planet with an atmosphere: by burning gigantic mountains of rocks, the oxygen and water that Jupiter had had in ancient times were released.

And now, when the decisive step of his excellent career was to take place before the planet Saturn ...

"Sorry, professor. He should never have listened to me!

"Bah! Don't worry, Jerry. Deep down, he already wanted to rest. I'm going to fish for trout in a river in Canada.

"But you have dedicated your whole life to ...

"There is! I have dedicated my entire life to space conquest, yearning to help men dominate at least the entire solar system. My dream has been that ... And I confess that it still is! An old man like me, with so much accumulated experience, can be of no use to anything else. But if "they" ...

He stopped when he saw that the young man who was listening wanted to speak. Jerry Kelly only took into account at that moment the damage that Walter Lehman could suffer and noted:

"I personally know Mr. Charles Wilder, professor. He was a great friend of my father, whom he met when he became one of the twelve wise men of the Wilder Institute. Maybe if I could talk to him ...

The elderly astrophysicist smiled gratefully, although inquiring:

"Do you have confidence in that man, Jerry?

"You see, Mr. Lehman... I once thought I was linked in some way to him. Her daughter, Fanny Wilder, is the one who ... I was going to marry her.

"Wow, boy! I didn't know such a thing. And how did the powerful Charles Wilder not help you in your investigations?

"He was always opposed, since my father died in them. You will already know that Charles Wilder is a very enterprising man, who likes to help people very much. His grandfather founded the Wilder Institute to help science, and he has followed the family tradition by endowing it with large sums. But a thousand times he told me that what my father was dreaming was nonsense. Acoustics does not interest him; Charles Wilder prefers to see the name of the institute linked to the conquest of any other planet.

Jerry Kelly seemed to recall as he continued:

"We have been arguing lately, at my insistence. Perhaps that was what affected my relationships with your daughter and I ... Well, professor, I applied for this position, as I already told you when I arrived, to continue investigating. The "Saturn XI" is an ideal platform, since it is so far from Earth.

"I appreciate your intention, Jerry, but it's too late now. The Investigative Commission is arriving. I didn't think they did in view of the report I sent. In it he detailed all the progress made in your project and the magnificent results that could be obtained. I put a lot of effort into this because I ... I firmly believe in your dream, Jerry!

Walter Lehman got up very lively for his years, clinching, with an energetic gesture:

"It's more, boy! Until I am officially relieved of my command post, no one will destroy what you have assembled on the Saturn XI.

"Destroy you say, Mr. Lehman? "Repeated, alarmed, the young acoustics specialist.

"That's right, Jerry. Days ago I received an order to dismantle your laboratory, with the excuse that all that material used can be adapted to other functions. I didn't want to say anything to you, in case things calmed down, but ... "his hand again pointed to the order received." You see!

"They seem to have a special interest in impeding my investigations, Professor. It is absurd that, since we have managed to assemble all that excellent equipment, now ...

"That's why I'll stop it! And if they process me ... they process me!

"No, Mr. Lehman. I will take responsibility for everything. I can't let you ...

Jerry Kelly stopped when he saw the gigantic radar screen attached to the back wall of the office lit up. The coordinates were pointing to an increasingly visible point, and after pressing the corresponding button on the control panel, Walter Lehman inquired through the visophone:

"What is it, Gassman?

An impersonal voice reached them:

"Sir ... the mothership is approaching. He said that it will be located while launching the vehicle in which the Investigative Commission will arrive.

"Good, Gassman. Order platform number three to be arranged. But that damned Peter Masson could get close, instead of sending all those gentlemen.

The same voice announced:

"General Masson said that they should bring supplies to the space base 'Mercury'. They will be located in the same place again, to receive the vehicle with those of the Commission and ...

"Drop it now, Gassman! "Urged the person in charge of the« Saturn XI ».

And with you, sir.

The intercom snapped shut as the astrophysicist met Jerry Kelly's gaze and exclaimed:

"You heard! They don't want to waste time.

Then he pressed another button, and when one of the panels of the office opened, he was in communication with his assistants, who remained in the adjoining room. The second in charge of the "Saturn XI" advanced towards his boss, and Walter Lehman announced:

"You will have to take over command, Anthony. I won't see those pretty rings from that damned planet again for two hours.

"Are they coming, professor?

"Yes, Anthony. They are coming!

Jerry Kelly was feeling overwhelmed. He was confused and did not know what to say to the man who, by helping him, believing in him and showing him his trust, after more than half a century of constant active service was about to see his magnificent career cut short.

CHAPTER V

A tall, inordinately thin man with a nervous tic that made the left corner of his thin lips pucker up, announced:

"I am Armstrong ... Roger Armstrong, in charge of this Investigative Commission, Professor Lehman.

Walter Lehman looked with tired eyes at the four individuals that the man presented with the fan movement of his hand, inclining his gray head slightly out of courtesy. Jerry Kelly did the same, as did his most direct collaborators: the blond Michel Sauet, the Herculean Arthur Hadmond, the electronic engineer Ramy Piccole, Billy Laughton and the graceful Dr. Marlene Power.

All of them felt as if they were accused, as they continued to listen to the somewhat cracked and metallic voice of that Roger Armstrong, who continued:

"Our visit is very unpleasant, but in view of what you have been doing on the 'Saturn XI', very precise. You must not have forgotten, especially you, Professor Lehman, that the program does not admit modifications or ...

"Nobody has modified anything, Mr. Armstrong" rectified, also, the cold voice of the old astrophysicist. Analyzes, measurements and surveys on Saturn have continued at their normal pace. I rely on the reports that Peter Masson must have received from time to time on his mothership.

"But they've gotten into some serious acoustic research, using this base as a platform for something that wasn't on the show.

"I insist on telling you that your boss, Peter Masson, knew about it. I communicated it to him as soon as I decided that Jerry Kelly was asking to do this extra work to continue his rehearsals.

"Let me personally remind Mr. Kelly that these trials and experiments were interrupted at the Wilder Institute with the unfortunate death of his father. Mr. Charles Wilder himself told him that ...

"I did not believe that the Wilder Institute opposed my continuing to investigate here" objected the aforementioned.

"You see, yes; As soon as information about the case has reached Earth, we have received an order to suspend them.

"May I ask why, Mr. Armstrong?

"Your question is a leading one, Mr. Kelly. In the case of such valuable material that you have had to use, you should know that this loss, in itself, constitutes a serious crime.

"It is no loss. Someday...

Roger Armstrong's thin, extremely bony hand moved in the air as he caught:

"If your program is ever approved, I and General Peter Masson will be the first to congratulate you, Mr. Kelly. But for now, we must vigorously oppose it. All your valuable laboratory will be transferred to the vehicle that you have brought us, to be taken to General Masson's mothership.

Again his hand waved to prevent them from taking advantage of the breath he took, warning:

"And all of you are relieved of your posts, including, of course, Professor Walter Lehman, who I hope has no objection.

"If they are superior orders, I will have to accept them, Mr. Armstrong.

"They are, professor. You can see the signature of General Masson for yourself. I know he is his friend, but if he is pressed too, he will understand that our duty is ...

He left the words hanging, and Jerry Kelly objected:

"Does my laboratory need to be dismantled, Mr. Armstrong?"

"Totally necessary! This Commission has been trained precisely for that, while at the same time it values all the instruments used in its proper measure. I understand that you have required many instruments of your own making.

"That's how it is. It has cost us a lot to design them, and even more to achieve them. Bear in mind that the role they are to perform has never been attempted until now. Even my father couldn't conceive for half the years. A few years ago the current techniques were not available, nor perhaps the poor man could find as good collaborators as I have been fortunate to find.

Jerry Kelly said this, indicating to the five men and the blonde girl who were next to him, who, despite giving the visitors the best of their smiles, heard Roger Armstrong reply, as if with visible satisfaction:

"Well, it's a shame all that work, Mr. Kelly

Then he turned to the four men who accompanied him, ordering them:

"They can start. I want a good inventory, painstakingly detailed piece by piece.

That same day, Jerry Kelly's collaborators gathered in the dining room, with great disgust he learned that, after the inventory, all his instruments were being packed, to be transported to the space vehicle with which they would depart, themselves also, towards the mothership.

Vehemently and unable to contain himself any longer, the Herculean Arthur Hadmond proposed:

"Is there no way to stop it, Jerry?

"Don't be gross! "Michel Sauet objected." How? Fucking with those idiots from the Investigative Commission?

"Why not?

"Because we would not anticipate anything, Arthur" Jerry Kelly soothed them.

Also resigned in part, Marlene Power opined:

"In a few days the mothership will be waiting for us. If we refuse to ship those devices and we don't go ...

"Don't think any more nonsense! Billy Laughton chimed in. That would be an uprising, and we've already gotten poor Professor Lehman in quite a bit of trouble.

Ramy Piccole had said nothing since dinner ended, but he abandoned his silence as he inquired, looking one by one at his friends:

"Do you think they will send us to Earth?

"That would not be a punishment" opined Arthur Hadmond.

The incognito was cleared the next day, when when taking over from the post that Jerry Kelly had « signed, his partner who was leaving the shift wished him:

"You are going to need a lot of luck, Jerry. So far no one has tried!

Jerry Kelly went to turn on the acoustic sounding machine to pick up the sound waves coming from the mass of the planet Saturn, when it was interrupted when inquiring:

"What do you mean, Sydney?

"To the rings. You have not heard?

"I come from my cabin now. By the way, I haven't slept much. I have spent the night thinking about our transfer, possibly to Earth.

Sydney made a puzzled face as she repeated:

"To the earth? But if you go to the rings! Captain Quiin told me! You are already preparing your spaceship.

"How do you say Sydney?

"That's right, Jerry. On platform number five; By the way, I don't know what all those machines that you've had Marlene, Arthur and the others build are going to do for you.

Even more astonished, Jerry Kelly left his post by asking:

"Can you go on for a couple more hours, Sydney? I want to confirm all that you say. I need to speak to Professor Lehman!

Sydney resumed her position, accepting compassionately:

"You can go, Jerry. A guy who's going to try to land somewhere in Saturn's rings, he can be allowed anything. It's like when you are sentenced to death and ...

"Do you want to shut up, Sydney?

Minutes later, Jerry Kelly was at the nerve center of that wonderful steel mechanic that was the artificial satellite "Saturn XI." Before him was again the elderly professor Walter Lehman, who confirmed to his questions:

"That's right, Jerry... let's try it!

"I have nothing to object, if I have been chosen, Professor Lehman. When I accepted this position, I knew what I was exposing myself to. But I would like to know if my designation, and yours as well, have something to do with the other.

"It must be so, boy, as the crew has included Arthur, Michel, Ramy, Billy and also ... Marlene Power too!

Jerry Kelly almost jumped as he advanced to the table another step, exclaiming:

"She too?

"Yes, Jerry... That poor girl, too!

"But why? Why all this, Mr. Lehman?

"I don't know, son. The order came directly from General Peter Masson.

Helplessly, the young man shook his fingers as he exclaimed:

"Well, yes, his good friend Masson loves him! Do you know what sends you to certain death?

"He must have received orders in turn, Jerry.

"Why did that Roger Armstrong say in the first place that he was going back to the mothership with us, those guys with him and all the instruments in my lab?

"He believed it that way too. The other order has come later.

"Agree! I know that one day or another you had to try. But he did not explain to me why precisely the six of us included in Captain Quiin's crew must go.

Jerry Kelly paced the spacious room nervously, hands clasped behind his back, as he continued, in view of the old man's silence:

"And much less explain to me that they have to load all my equipment onto Captain Quiin's spacecraft. What good can it be there, if we are not sure whether or not we will be able to make contact in those doomed rings?

Almost with a small voice, Walter Lehman stated:

"We won't be able, Jerry... I am more and more convinced that they do not form a solid platform. They are condensations of bases! And poisonous gases!

"I admit that someone has to come up one day to confirm that or deny it, professor. But I can't believe that our appointment was a "coincidence"!

The astrophysicist got up slowly saying:

"I'm not afraid of death either, Jerry. At my age, after having seen so much and having come out well in many other circumstances, that does not count.

His voice grew more energetic and changed tone as he exclaimed:

"But it revolts me that they send us there as if they wanted ..., as if they were trying to get rid of us!

Jerry Kelly was silent, respecting his boss's muffled anger. He knew that frankly he would continue to present everything he thought to him and he was not surprised to hear him add:

"What the hell! Our crime has not been that serious. What? Are those millions that we have spent on instruments, material and machinery worth more than our lives?

"It's not that way, Mr. Lehman. The fact that these instruments are being loaded onto Captain Quiin's ship proves it. Even if they risk our lives Exploring space, especially the unknown, you know better than anyone that it always involves risk. But ... why wear all that? Do you think we are going to find an ideal place to land and settle in so that I can continue my research?

"I said, Jerry. They want to get rid of us of all that!

"But ... who, professor? Your friend, General Peter Masson?

"I don't know ... I'm confused! Peter and I have always had good friends. It's hard for me to believe that the order came from him!

"Have you communicated directly with General Masson, sir?

"I could not. He entered the order by code, with all his security requirements, but they told me he was not on the mothership. There is a space base that required your visit.

Jerry Kelly was silent, but his mind did not stop working. In a few seconds he thought of many things. In the risky journey that he would have to make, in which he would be accompanied, in his beloved instruments that had cost him many years of work, tenacity and effort to imagine.

For now, now that they had finally gotten them ...

Aloud, he only stated:

"Poor Marlene! He's so young ...

"Her presence on the expedition they say is justified by being a great specialist in Cybernetics. General Masson's code order specifically indicated that it should be included in case once there we were forced to improvise. That girl is very bright and ...

Without really knowing why, Jerry Kelly suddenly knew:

"And what do those of that brand-new Investigative Commission say? It would have made them feel like a shot to be included in that little trip too!

"Roger Armstrong went white and his lip began to tremble with that nervous tic that usually seems to make him pucker up," the astrophysicist said, something amusing.

"Are you specialists in something, Mr. Lehman?

"No, but the order indicated that they could cover secondary ports. After all, they are all men properly trained for life in space.

They fell silent again, broken by Jerry's voice who wanted to confirm:

"When do we leave, professor?

Walter Lehman had the strange and annoying feeling that it was he who sentenced his friends by pointing out: in a quiet voice:

"First thing tomorrow morning, son ...

CHAPTER VI

Arthur Hadmond looked out through the transparent quartz window, saying, in his loud booming voice:

"Who was the fool who sang to the brightness of the sky, to its pure" blue ", to all those trifles?

"It must have been some poet", Michel Sauet clarified reluctantly.

"Well, I see it black! Black as bitumen! Better yet, guys. Like a wolf's mouth!

"That's what it is, Arthur. A wolf's mouth that will devour us!

All eyes were focused on the one who had said something that, deep down, they confessed it or not, everyone thought. They had been thinking about it since takeoff platform number 5 had been ready, launching Captain Marty Quiin's spaceship into space.

The "Saturn XI" was left behind, until it became a luminous and brilliant point, as if it were one of the ten natural satellites of the unknown planet whose neighborhood they had to explore.

Ramy Piccole caught the eye of his fellow scouts and protested, after the heavy silence behind his last words:

"What's happening? Why do you look at me like that? Did I say nonsense?

"You did, Ramy.

After saying this, Jerry Kelly left his seat after loosening the belts, approaching Marlene Power to ask:

"You want to help me? It will be necessary to make some modifications to the radiation meter. I see the numbers keep increasing.

Reluctantly, the blonde woman denied:

"I don't really want to work, Jerry. And if you're doing it to keep her entertained and not listen to Ramy's bad omens, don't bother. Don't think anything I say affects me!

"Well. To me, yes! "Protested, for his part, Michel Sauet." What an idiot! It is not pleasant that you are constantly reminding you that you may die.

"Cretin! "Replied the aforementioned dryly, standing next to the tall Arthur, to also look outside.

Nerves were unleashed and Michel Sauet quickly broke free of the straps, being stopped by the elderly Walter Lehman, who advised:

"Why isn't everyone trying to stay calm? Or are they going to tell me that this is the first time they have made a risky trip?

"A risky trip, no, professor" snapped Ramy Piccole sulkily. But I had never been ordered to commit suicide! And you know we'll disintegrate as we get close to those damned rings!

"I'm not sure, Ramy. This is what you have to try!

"Oh yeah? Are we guinea pigs? Why precisely with a manned ship? I remember in the first soundings of Jupiter ...

"There it is, boy! "He cut him off, hoping to be a catalyst for everyone's nerves." Do you really remember that?

"It cannot be easily forgotten, Mr. Lehman. Come on ... It seems to me!

"Well, you will also remember that when the first remote-controlled ships were sent, we all thought they would not arrive. And they arrived!

"This is different, friend. Look at the radiation meter! Do you think that needle has gone crazy?

Jerry Kelly insisted, inviting the woman:

Come on, Marlene. The mechanism may be wrong. We must program it to resist greater influences. It's a matter of...

The blonde girl followed him, sliding down the central staircase to the lower level. The spacecraft led by Captain Marty Quiin was not large. Everything was in place to make the most of the space, and although the entire crew could stay in it for half a year, it could not be said that there was half a cubic meter left over.

On the ground floor was the general room, and there the unpleasant Roger Armstrong met them, who came up announcing:

"Come on, Jerry. There is something I want you to see!

"What is it, Mr. Armstrong? Are you also excited?

"There is to be, believe me.

They followed him through the narrow metal corridors, until they reached the warehouse. Seeing all his packed instruments lined up there, Jerry Kelly couldn't help but say

"Pity! With all that it cost us to build this, I don't know what they are going to do for us now!

Roger Armstrong approached one of the packages, putting his hands on it, announcing:

"You're welcome, because these are not your Jerry instruments.

"How do you say? Marlene intervened, as surprised as her young companion.

What they hear. I have opened one of these packages and checked it. Someone tricked us! And I would like to know why!

Feverishly, Jerry Kelly's hands began to rip the waterproofed tarp off the bundles. They contained tools, computers, counters, and all kinds of instruments.

But they were not the ones who with so much effort, work and love he had ordered to build his friends!

The blonde woman's big blue eyes searched his and her voice inquired:

"What do you think this could mean, Jerry?

"First of all, a hoax, Marlene.

"But from who?

"It's the first thing we have to find out.

Roger Armstrong kept exposing the packaging, yelling, almost in a fit of hysteria:

"Look! Check this out! They are useless machines. Many are missing parts. They have been put in place of their instruments!

Then, calmer, he stopped going from one package to another, adding:

"I came here out of curiosity, and remembering the apparatus that you had shown me on the 'Saturn XI', I saw that they were not yours. Someone had them loaded onto Captain Quiin's ship, instead of the others!

"Which means that yours are still on the" Saturn XI "" deduced the woman.

"That's it, Marlene. But who could do such a thing?

"My question is: And why? Roger Armstrong said again.

The three were silent as they pondered. At last Jerry Kelly's markedly manly voice thought aloud:

"I fear that...

"What, Jerry? Speak Please!

"Yes, Marlene... I think I should, even if it seems crazy and monstrous. I start to tie details together and they lead me to this conclusion: "Someone" wants to get rid of us. From all the team we have formed!

He paused, before continuing:

"They send us, by higher order, to explore the rings of Saturn because they hope we will not return!

"But your instruments ...

"There is! They have led us to believe that the order also included them and that they should be loaded onto this spacecraft ... But it is not like that! Which indicates that they are still in "Saturn XI" ... Because that "someone" is interested.

Tall and thin Roger Armstrong's bony hand was raised, warning:

"And why have they included us in the exploration? I chaired the Investigative Commission that should ...

"That's why Mr. Armstrong! "Jerry stopped him." You and the four men who accompany you also knew something of what I proposed to do and also ... you also wish to see them eliminated!

"Who, Jerry? Are you thinking of General Peter Masson, the mothership's commander-in-chief?

"He sent you, didn't he?

"Yes, but General Masson has always been an honest man, incapable of such a thing. What interest can he have that ...?

"If we continue in this suicidal exploration, we will never be able to find out. I'm going to talk to Captain Quiin!

"Wait, Jerry! Are you going to tell him not to continue the journey?

"Exactly, friend!

"But that... that is disobeying orders! It's as much as ...

"This justifies us. There is already an anomaly in our expedition, and we are not going to wait for any excuse to be given to us over the radio. We will return to the "Saturn XI" there we will find out who it was that made the change are these packages.

"It must have been Louis Streisand! He is in charge of loading and unloading the "Saturn XI"! When they send us supplies and material from the mothership, it is he who receives it, just like when Professor Lehman had to send something to General Masson or to Earth.

"Well, that Louis Streisand will have to explain this to us," Jerry Kelly said firmly.

"It will be necessary to speak with the others, Jerry.

"We will, Marlene. After all, Professor Walter Lehman is still our boss.

* * *

One of Captain Marty Quiin's crewmen approached his boss and must have whispered something quietly in his ear.

Captain Quiin looked at everyone assembled, seemed to take a breath, and finally announced:

"Friends ... There is more than just a change of packaging! Sergeant Evans just told me that, searching the warehouse well, they have found a "nice" device that can make us fly at any moment.

He saw alarm and surprise on all faces, focusing his gaze on the blonde woman as he soothed:

"They should not worry. My men are beginning to disassemble that little atomic charge. And I hope they get it!

Roger Armstrong began to stir around, like a thin eel being pulled out of the water. The comments began and the ship's commander's voice asked again:

"Don't be upset! If we act calmly, I think we can return to "Saturn XI."

"Is it already decided, Captain? "Asked one of Roger Armstrong's four companions.

It was the voice of the elderly astrophysicist Walter Lehman that replied:

"Given all this, we are not going to continue with the exploration. I bear the responsibility! I'll get in touch with General Masson and ...

"May I, professor?

Walter Lehman fixed his tired eyes on Jerry Kelly's face, who continued at his consent:

"Better to do it on our own, professor. More prudent!

"But is it that... you think Peter Masson can...?

"We can always say that the intercom broke down. Once back on "Saturn XI," Louis Streisand will have to tell us about the change in those packages ... and how that "nice gift that Captain Quiin's men found there got into the cargo!"

"They wanted to volatilize us! Exclaimed Ramy Piccole

He faced as soon as he gave his exclamation to Michel Sauet, reminding him:

"Didn't you call me a bird of ill omen? Well, see if I had a good nose!

"Please" asked the commander of the ship. Stop arguing. I beg you each to take your place and let my crew sort that out.

It was the tall, Herculean Arthur Hadmond who started the exit, muttering:

"If I find out who the criminal is who wanted to send us to hell ..., I will strangle him with my bare hands!

CHAPTER VII

Before starting the first orbit around "Saturn XI", the order came from the planet's artificial satellite to Captain Marty Quiin's spacecraft:

"Identify yourselves! This is "Saturn XI"! Identify yourselves!

Manning the spacecraft, Captain Quiin looked back to meet the gaze of astrophysicist Walter Lehman and young Jerry Kelly. At last he connected the intercom, transmitting:

"This is" Delta-5. " The ship commanded by Captain Marty Quiin. We return to base! Permission to land.

The voice reached them perfectly audible and sharp:

"Denied! You have a mission to fulfill. They should be ten million kilometers from here!

Walter Lehman stepped forward, and it was he who replied:

"Gassman? It's me, Walter Lehman. I gave you command of the "Saturn XI" by order of General Peter Masson ... Good. I return and take command of the "Saturn XI" again. And we are going to land! We need platform number five to be put in a position to ...

A series of interferences announced to them that the answer was colliding with the sound waves of their message. The astrophysicist was silent to finally be able to capture:

"What is this all about, Professor Lehman? I have a responsibility and I insist that you ...

"It's an order, Gassman! A case of extreme emergency!

"Good teacher. I'll give the order for platform number five to be set up.

Two hours later, Captain Marty Quiin's spacecraft was sliding down the gigantic ramp that would take them into the hangars of the "Saturn XI." Everyone had the feeling that this was like going "home." In that gigantic artificial satellite they had spent more than a year and there they would have all the comforts that during that short exploration trip they had had to do without.

Furthermore, they were all eager to know the causes because, in a deliberate and criminal way, they had been sent to their deaths.

A death that later could have been justified, claiming that the expedition to the rings of the planet Saturn had been a failure.

Marty Quiin was performing the maneuver with his usual skill, when suddenly he sensed on the controls that something was wrong. He quickly glanced at the dashboard and saw that ramp number 5 was beginning to close prematurely.

This was absurd.

No one could be so clumsy on the "Saturn XI" to initiate the closing operation before the end of the maneuver. Instinctively, Marty Quiin started the engines, getting ahead of him in turn so as not to be swept away by the closing of that gigantic ramp of hard steel, as if they were an insect.

They slid down the ramp almost vertically and the crash was tremendous. The formidable weight of the spacecraft destroyed part of the hangars, a thousand sparks arose from the short circuits and a fire broke out in one of them.

The automatic alarm began to buzz and in the corridors of the "Saturn XI" all was activity and movement.

And suddenly, Captain Marty Quiin's ship tore apart as if a formidable force were ripping it apart ...

* * *

The first thing Jerry Kelly saw again was beautiful blue eyes gazing at him. He was still feeling half dazed, but he thought he guessed in those woman's eyes, love; at least they gazed upon him with infinite sweetness.

He managed to sit up and, perplexed, inquired:

"Where am I, Marlene?

"In the infirmary. Fortunately, you only suffered one concussion.

"What happened?

"They say there was an accident.

Then, more quietly, he announced:

"It cost more than twenty deaths, Jerry. Poor Arthur, Michel and Ramy, too ...

"And Professor Lehman?

"It is also being cared for. There are more than thirty injured.

"So many?

"Yes; Among those of us who were returning, the hangar personnel and Captain Quiin's crew ... Many doubt they can be saved. A fire broke out and ... It was horrible!

Jerry Kelly stayed seated, mostly to see if he could move. His pajama jacket exposed his broad, hairy thorax, and the blonde woman asked:

"You must not move now, Jerry.

"I feel fine. I want to talk as soon as possible | with Professor Lehman and with Gassman.

"I have seen him; I've told you everything, but ...

"Go on, Marlene.

"Louis Streisand has also died. Apparently, he was the one who operated the lever so that ramp number five closed before finishing the maneuver. What he shouldn't have counted on was poor Captain Quiin's quick reaction. He fired the engines and managed to slide the ship inside. But in the clash, he too ...

Jerry Kelly was silent, and Marlene Power continued to report:

"Apparently one of the engines exploded. The fire spread to the hangars and that scoundrel ...

"Why would Louis Streisand do all that?

"We can never find out anymore. Gassman doesn't know why he changed the packaging, causing the crew to load onto Captain Quiin's ship other packages that did not contain your instruments.

"So... are you still here, Marlene?

The blonde woman seemed to hesitate before reporting:

"No, Jerry ... Gassman says that during our absence another ship from the mother approached with orders to take them away.

"Wow! That implies a coordinated collusion. They send us off "Saturn XI", load other packages onto the ship that has to carry out this exploration, leave my instruments here, and when they believe us in hell ... others come and take them away!

"So it was, Jerry.

"Has Gassman told you by order of whom?

"By order of General Peter Masson.

"I supposed!

"Are you going to get up?

"Yes, Marlene. I have too many things to do to stay here! If you go out for a moment, I ...

A nurse in a white coat approached, also protesting:

"You must not get up, Mr. Kelly. The doctor said that you ...

"I feel fine, miss. Do you two want to leave the room?

Half an hour later, at the command post of the "Saturn XI", Jerry Kelly found the elderly astrophysicist Walter Lehman, speaking with his assistant Gassman.

Lehman had his right arm in a sling, with a bandage around his head that covered his wild gray hair. He did not get up when he saw him enter, but he said, with a half smile:

"Nice to see you well, Jerry. I've been explaining everything to Gassman.

Jerry Kelly felt some discomfort in his left side, no doubt from his body being hit there when the spacecraft exploded. But he tried to forget himself and, pointing to the intercom, wanted to know:

"Have you contacted General Masson?

"No, Jerry ... I remembered what you said. It is more prudent to act on our own!

"I celebrate it, professor. I'm beginning to suspect that General Masson is involved in all of this.

"I have a hard time believing it, son. Peter has always been a good friend of mine!

"Yes... but he sent him to lead an expedition that was doomed! And not only that, Mr. Lehman. Someone put a criminal device there to atomize us!

"All that is inexplicable" spoke Gassman.

"The facts sing. Have you taken any action?

Gassman had already handed over command to his old boss, but replied:

"Yes: the interior security police are investigating.

"With results?

"Not until now; All warehouse personnel claim that Louis Streisand ordered them to load their instruments onto Captain Quiin's ship. But apparently the packages contained others.

Jerry Kelly looked at him questioningly as he said;

"This won't work, Gassman ... After we left the 'Saturn XI', another vehicle arrived here from the mothership. And they came with an order to take my gadgets!

"True, but... what could I do?

"At least one thing. Investigate why someone had given them the change!

Looking visibly weary, the elderly Walter Lehman intervened:

"You could have made another one, Gassman: we warned.

"Hey! Are they now going to accuse me of something? I did not know that...

Jerry Kelly's voice was commanding when ordering, seeing that Gassman began to get up:

"Sit down! And if I were Professor Lehman, I'd order him to be detained until this mess was cleared up.

"Stop me?

"Yes, 'friend' ... All these manipulations of loading and unloading could not have been done without your knowledge. It is very cumbersome to pack more than five tons of material, not to say that it is practically impossible to have a small atomic bomb like the one we found as a "gift" on Captain Quiin's ship. With Professor Lehman handing over command to you, "Saturn XI" has been under your control, and you're not going to tell me that Louis Streisand had access to the secret department where these artifacts are kept, are you, Gassman?

"Is this a formal accusation?

Take it as you like. You have always aspired to fill the position of Professor Walter Lehman. And this was an excellent opportunity!

"The transmission of command came from a higher order. General Masson did the same.

"That is another problem that we will have to fix.

"Are you planning to get out of" Saturn XI "again?

Again in a tired voice, Walter Lehman confirmed:

"We will, Gassman. I'm not going to clear up all this over the radio with Peter. I need to speak to him personally! I'm afraid this whole conspiracy has come from somewhere and I want to know how far it goes. There are many lives lost and many more at stake!

Gassman finally got to his feet, already wielding a "Lasser" beam weapon that he had been craftily searching one of the table's drawers. His face seemed transfigured and he yelled at them:

"No one will get out of here!

"Gassman! Then then ... Jerry is right! You're in on this!

"Yes, you crazy old man. But they will never know where the shots are coming from! Have you ever thought that you are too many years old to enjoy a position like the one you had? What did he aspire to? To conquer the entire solar system? It was there when the Mars and Jupiter thing. Now it's my turn! I have worked hard so that my name is linked to that of Saturn. And this program will be me who will carry it forward!

"You are blinded by ambition, Gassman... You have murdered many people!

"Do not! Not that! Louis Streisand caused the ramp accident.

"With your consent! Before all the personnel of the «Saturn XI» you would remain as innocent. You allowed us to get closer ... But to fall into that trap!

"He also knew the 'little gift' we carried on Captain Quiin's ship," Jerry Kelly objected.

"Agree! "Ended up admitting." That's why I can't care about a couple more deaths.

And what will he say? What had to strike us down with that "Lasser" right here?

"I'll find something" convincing. " Don't worry, dear Jerry!

"You are a dirty assassin, Gassman! For years I have taught you everything I knew.

Gassman glared at the old man, roaring at him:

"Yes! Always as a second! Me doing all the work, carrying everything on my head, always exhausting myself so that the glory would go to you. Didn't you realize?

"I admit I may have overworked you, but that's no reason to hate me so much, Gassman.

"I don't hate you, man. It just gets in the way! Little by little he was delegating his functions to me and that has made me get used to the command. Why not do it all alone, without his shadow? You can't handle panties anymore, Mr. Lehman! I've been saying it to everyone like that!

"Is that because of Peter Masson's order? Did you tell the general that he could no longer be in command here?

"Exactly, old man! Did you worry about intercoms? I also spoke to Earth about those acoustic investigations that your good friend Jerry made you agree to do here. Cast.,. That was precisely what made me open my eyes! You committed an abuse: the Wilder Institute should know about it. That center carries all the Saturn programming and ...

"Go on! Jerry Kelly urged, so keenly interested he forgot the death threat hanging over them.

But Gassman grinned crookedly as he cackled:

"Ah, no, friend! I told him that I would go to hell without knowing anything. You will not be the one to make "The Voice of the Universe" speak! It will be another! Another much more powerful and with more rights!

And the murderous hand that wielded the deadly weapon aimed at its first victim.

Jerry Kelly had no doubt that at that moment he was going to die.

CHAPTER VIII

That is why he thought that if he died, it was best to do it fighting.

He flexed his legs hard, throwing himself across the table at his rival, who in turn also sprang into action. The "Lasser" beam shot from the weapon with a click that briefly illuminated the office. The beam of light went straight to where Jerry Kelly had been just seconds ago; but there it did not trip over the man's body to pierce him, scorching him with its deadly power.

Gassman was gripped by the neck as another iron paw pressed against the wrist of the armed hand. A second click announced another jet of deadly light, but this time too the Lasser struck the ceiling, as metallic as the floor.

He left his mark there, as the fingers of Jerry Kelly's right hand sank lower and lower, mad desperation down that throat. Driven by his frenzy, always eager to disable such a dangerous enemy, he did not realize that Gassman was no longer struggling and was dropping the weapon. They had rolled on the floor of the office, in a confused heap of bodies, legs and arms.

When he withdrew his hand, he understood what he had done.

That crazy and ambitious murderer no longer lived. Jerry Kelly had strangled him by breaking him with the formidable pressure of her fingers, by dropping all her weight on him, the tiny bones of his throat.

Walter Lehman leaned over the man who had been his chief aide, muttering:

"He deserved it, Jerry... You don't have to feel sorry for killing him.

"The only thing I feel is that I cannot say more things. But I couldn't stop squeezing! He had that gun in his hand and you know what could have happened if one of us had been hit.

The elderly astrophysicist looked down at the ground, where the metal had melted like butter from the powerful beam of Lasser. On the ceiling there was also another similar sign and making affirmative signs with the bandaged head still whispered:

"Be careful, we men invent things! And many of them for evil!

He walked around the tumbled table, pressed a button, and as the face of the nurse on duty appeared on the visophone screen, Walter Lehman ordered:

"Tell Dr. Matthaus to come over, miss. Ah! And with two nurses and a stretcher.

"Yes, Professor Lehman.

Communication was cut off and the astrophysicist asked the young man that I watched him:

"Can you take the trip with me, Jerry?

"Yes, teacher. I only suffered a few bumps and bruises. When will we leave for the mothership?

"The sooner the better. Rabio for meeting Peter Masson!

* * *

The artificial satellite "Saturn XI" was a matchbox compared to the gigantic dimensions of the mothership.

He had been on active duty for more than twelve years and had not suffered a single minor breakdown. All its complicated mechanisms worked perfectly: its builders could be satisfied.

And proud of having created that mechanical marvel, an artificial world that traveled from one planet to another, like a true nurse capable of feeding countless "suckers" located in the most distant and capricious orbits.

The Wilder Institute had achieved deserved fame, after the financing and construction of that gigantic mobile space station, capable of accommodating more than five thousand human beings, which in turn served fifty spaceships in charge of distributing the necessary supplies throughout the world. Solar system.

The mothership was the center of an invisible spider web stretched out in space, where the comings and goings of the ships that departed or arrived at it braided the threads of interplanetary travel, in a constant weaving and unweaving of those sidereal communications of men.

The most modern electronic brains programmed, without a single fault, those transfers of the spaceships from one place to another. Not the smallest detail was left to chance, everything running to the tenth of a second, controlled by their atomic clocks. At any moment you knew what was going to happen: in the mothership there could be no mistakes, no faults, not the slightest mistake. Such a thing would mean that a ship rushing toward her would not find her in the right place. Or the other way around: that those who started from their launching pads had to make improvised tours.

And there was no improvisation at all.

The men in his crew had turned into machines.

Human machines that no longer had their own opinion, because the other machines created by him imposed them on them. Computers, electronic brains, devices created by the most modern and complicated cybernetics.

Cybernetics is, above all, a logical science, insofar as it rationally analyzes what it means to govern, without asking the question of knowing who governs or how it is governed, since the function of governing, of regulating, can be performed by machines. , provided that they are capable of capturing information about the status of a system and of preparing, based on the information received, orders that govern the subsequent orientation of the system. In this plane, it allows a vast theoretical classification of systems and machines, such as man had never undertaken before in his past.

Cybernetics is also the point of pairing of important applications, since its conclusions derive the possibility of building all kinds of governing and regulating machines, thus facilitating the tasks of man to infinity.

On the technique of automatic control systems, cybernetics was presented as a crossroads science for its own creators, developing general notions in relation to the mechanisms capable of governing and regulating all the necessary functions. This approach constituted the starting point of a vast movement, which could come to suppose a true intellectual revolution, which would include the logical analysis of the functions of higher beings and of the processes that allow them to be artificially reproduced.

Given this, some famous cybernetics held the opinion that social phenomena, insofar as they result from the exchange of information, could be studied using the methods of cybernetics, which would allow us to glimpse, in the field of a bold anticipation perspective, the image of a possible human society ruled by machines of thinking and governing.

Machines that did not have a single fault.

General Peter Masson himself was subjected to this iron discipline imposed by the machines, so he did not come out of his astonishment when from the checkpoint they announced that a spaceship was approaching them, whose trip had not been programmed.

He was puzzled for a while before ordering

"Identify yourself.

"You already did, General Masson.

Where does it come from? Is it an emergency?

"It comes from 'Saturn XI', sir. Apparently,its friend, Professor Walter Lehman, comes in it.

"Impossible! Walter must be close to Saturn's rings by now. You were given a mission!

"Do you want to come to the control room yourself, sir? "One of his assistants invited him.

With his rigid gait of lively and elastic steps, the massive General Peter Masson let the sliding tapes installed in all the corridors carry him. He only used his own energies when it was absolutely necessary and once in the control room he verified what he was told.

He spoke directly to Walter Lehman, but not a single friendly word escaped his lips at this unusual situation. Peter Masson always followed the rules and reading the schedule for that day did not indicate at all the unexpected arrival of that ship.

At last he turned away from the intercom to face a gigantic radar screen, where faint points of light indicated the space traffic in an area of twenty million kilometers. Before their manipulations the computers began to work, throwing data, figures, distances, schedules and all the operations that the mother ship would have to carry out in the next three days. The small cards were "swept" by a mechanical hand which in turn subjected them to data synthesis.

Peter Masson read the figures and turning to one of the assistants announced:

"Tell them they won't be able to enter the mothership for 77 hours, 55 minutes, and 26 seconds. Until then, all the controls are automated and none of the landing ramps would work to receive them.

"Well sir.

"Another thing: they must travel about six thousand miles so as not to interrupt the other scheduled entrances and exits. Even intercom will be cut with that ship. We cannot afford to alter our programming for them for a single minute!

Then, like a luxury in him, he quietly mused before returning to his office.

"Sorry! Say so to Professor Lehman.

"Yes Sir.

* * *

Walter Lehman looked despondently at his friends, exclaiming in summary:

"That's it!

Jerry Kelly felt Marlene Power's fingers squeeze his hand, falling along his body. They formed a circle in front of the elderly astrophysicist, who with his head bandaged and even his arm in a sling, each day that passed showed signs of being more exhausted.

Billy Laughton broke the silence by warning, reminding his friends:

"We have oxygen only for three more days, teacher. If you said that we must remain in orbit for about 80 hours, calculating the time of the maneuvers, they will tell me what we are going to breathe in those remaining 8 hours.

"I've already thought of that, Billy," said the old man. And we only have one solution left.

"Yes, of course, professor. Throw some of us down the hatch! For me we can cast it to luck.

Billy Laughton found Jerry Kelly's gaze not accepting that joke. Instantly he knew why his friend was reacting so seriously when he heard the old astrophysicist say:

"I'm not worth much anymore and I could ...

"Please, Professor Lehman! There is still another solution "the blonde girl cut him off.

All eyes were focused on Marlene Power, who in turn observed them one by one as she proposed:

"Hibernation! I have heard that a few years ago, an entire crew was saved by setting the automatic controls on their ship and voluntarily submitting to it. It is a physical state in which you do not breathe and ...

"Talk no more, Marlene! Jerry decided for everyone.

"We can draw lots for that! "Billy Laughton insisted again." At least, I don't like it at all to stay stuck like a corpse in a glass urn. What do you think?

The ship's commander was present and broke his silence by announcing:

"I will speak to the men of my crew. I think I will be able to do without some of them and in this way we will have more oxygen.

Only when he left the cabin did he protest, visibly upset:

"I don't know when they are going to install constant oxygen regeneration on these ships! It is time to make up your mind!

This was one of the many technical problems to be solved, at least for normal spaceships.

The man had accomplished many things. But he still had so many more to achieve.

It is your constant task, which never ends.

Perhaps because constant laws of life require it so.

CHAPTER IX

General Peter Masson listened silently to Walter Lehman, not once interrupting him.

Only at the end of his long story, the head of the mothership denied:

"Here we don't know anything about that ship that Gassman told him was in my name looking for those acoustic instruments.

The elderly astrophysicist inquired puzzled:

"How do you say, Peter?

"You heard me! You know my specific orders: they were that you should, with Jerry Kelly, Billy Laughton, Ramy Piccole, Michel Sauet, Arthur Hadmond and Marlene Power, to explore the rings of Saturn. I included that Roger Armstrong and those accompanying him, who made up the Investigative Commission, should accompany you in Captain Marty Quiin's spaceship. That was it!

Coming out of his silence, Jerry Kelly dared to intervene:

"So my valuable instruments... They have been stolen!

"I cannot assure you, young man," General Masson replied. Nor do I have any news of any ship going to "Saturn XI" after you left.

"Gassman made it so," recalled Walter Lehman.

"From what he told us, that Gassman also had direct communications with Earth," the acoustic engineer returned.

"All that is secondary, Jerry" asked the wounded old man patiently.

He looked directly at his friend Peter Mason again and wanted to know, urging him:

"Why did you send us to the rings, Peter?

"I received the order from the Wilder Institute. They said that this exploration was included in the Saturn programming.

"True! But why precisely me, us? I mean Jerry, Marlene, Billy, Arthur ... All of us who, in one way or another, had collaborated in these acoustic investigations!

"You know very well that I never ask why the orders I receive. I limit myself to fulfilling them.

"I know, Peter. I know! Little by little you have become: an automaton.

"To be in charge of a position like mine, I have to do it that way.

"And don't feelings count for you?

"You have nothing to reproach me for, Walter! I admit that I felt a great sadness when I saw that you were one of those who had to carry out that risky exploration, but what could I do if your appointment came from the Wilder Institute itself?

"Excuse me, sir ..." Jerry objected again, "Do you mean that it was on Earth, at the Wilder Institute itself, where they chose all of us for that mission?

Facing him with some disgust, General Masson confirmed:

"Of course, young man! Don't think it was me!

Jerry Kelly seemed to forget about him to look at his friends when he exclaimed:

"We should have guessed! It is at the Wilder Institute where there must be someone interested in my not being able to finish my experiments. This is where they don't want to hear "The voice of the Universe."

"The voice of the Universe? General Masson repeated almost like an echo.

"We have given it that name," Jerry informed him. The most appropriate, because one day it will be a reality. Although they wish to interrupt my work!

"It is absurd to think that the Wilder Institute wants to hinder its work, when everyone knows that it sponsors the most audacious research. Mr. Wilder himself is in love with science.

"I know, General Masson" Jerry agreed. But there are many people and many high officials there. And my heart tells me that the low blows come from there!

"We will find out! "The old astrophysicist promised warmly." As soon as Peter provides us with one of his ships, we will return to Earth.

General Peter Masson seemed to put on his rigid and hermetic man's mask again, replying sharply to the old friend:

"Don't expect me to do that, Walter. Everything is programmed here!

"I know ... But you are the one who does that programming!

"You expect me to alter the whole system?

"What I hope is that the crimes do not go unpunished, my friend. More than twenty men have died and more than thirty are still wounded on the "Saturn XI". Many of them will not be able to save themselves: they suffer serious injuries and burns.

Jerry Kelly interjected again, in support of the elderly professor:

"Besides that, General Masson, it is necessary to unmask who is pulling the strings of this conspiracy. There is no doubt that it must be very powerful to be able to pull the strings, more than a billion kilometers from Earth, using ambitious men like Gassman, Louis Streisand and others who may be waiting to strike their low blows.

"Yes, young. That's true! The space must be free of crime and low interest. Only in this way, with a constant work full of righteousness, will we be able to conquer him completely one day.

He paused, looked at the old friend, and his features became less rigid as he continued:

"But they will have to wait for me to do my math. I cannot and should not alter the movement of entrances and exits just like that! If he did, there would be no one here to understand each other. Understand that I have a lot of responsibility on my shoulders! The crews of all

the spaceships that in their incessant coming and going have ...

"Don't try harder, Peter" begged his friend. We undertake you and we will know how to wait.

* * *

Watching the bustle from one of the walkways that led down a long corridor, Marlene Power exclaimed:

"They look like ants!

Jerry Kelly also looked at the men and women drifting along the conveyor belts along the aisle, confirming:

"Yes, Marlene: they have a four-hour work day, depending on the shifts. But they work hard!

"Would you like to be stationed here, Jerry?

"Psch! I've seen some pretty faces, but ...

"Oh! "She protested, feigning anger." Other than that, man.

"Well no; General Masson is a very rigid man. Too much for my temper!

"Everyone speaks highly of him.

"I guess he must be a good boss. Truth be told, I think I already miss Earth. In the entire solar system there is nothing like our old but beloved planet!

"I think that way too, Jerry. The space seems cold to me, without landscape and, in a way, monotonous.

"We are land creatures, Marlene. We are bound to miss our natural environment.

"It's true! I have always been horrified by the idea of having a child outside of Earth. I don't know, but ... Those who are born that way, I think they are very different from us.

Jerry Kelly leaned on the railing, muttering without looking at the woman:

"Has there been the possibility of getting married, while you were destined on" Saturn XI "?

Believe it or not, yes. I have been courted by many men!

"It's natural. You were the prettiest there.

"Should I take it as a compliment, or do you really think so? The woman said, even more flirtatiously.

Jerry Kelly defended himself by replying:

"I said there, not here.

Amused, he saw her pouting in disgust, clinching from the height of the railing that overlooked that corridor:

"Look at that brunette! She is very cute!

"Son, with those miniskirt uniforms that you wear, any woman is attractive. I don't know how General Masson allows them to ...

"Do you dislike it?

"Oh no! Recreate the view all you want, you rascal! For me...

The blonde woman wanted to change the conversation, inquiring as distracted:

"When do you think General Masson will allow us to leave?

"Depends on his blissful schedule. It does nothing without consulting their computers first.

Jerry Kelly was still leaning over the railing, but he turned his head at the feel of her hand on his shoulder. Marlene Power's big blue eyes looked sad when she inquired, with a new change of tone:

"Aren't you afraid that when you get to Earth something will happen to you, Jerry?

"We were at greater risk on the 'Saturn XI', in that poor Captain Quiin's ship, and it is possible that right here.

"But I think that if someone is very interested in foot, do not continue with your investigations, there ...

"Calm down, Marlene, all this must be clarified once and for all. And on Earth we can do it. The authorities will have to hear Professor Lehman's report.

"But he ... he ...

"He has told me that at his age he does not mind losing his position. He is already very tired! And as for the material that he allowed me to use ... I don't think they will prosecute him for that!

"By the way ... Where do you think all the gadgets we managed to build will be?" Who will have raised them?

"With Louis Streisand and Gassman dead, it will be very difficult to find out. But maybe we will too. Or we will build others!

Marlene Power ended up smiling, saying:

"You are an excellent friend, Jerry. You are always cuddly. I like men who never give up!

He took her female hands in his, searching her beautiful blue eyes as he answered:

"And I love pretty blondes like you, Marlene. Have I never told you that you are dangerously attractive?

"Me...? She protested, though amused.

"Yes, you... maddeningly suggestive!

"Don't make jokes. I know for a fact that you are still in love with a woman.

It was his turn to surprise him, almost denying it.

"Me...?

"Yes, you ..." she remedied, with the same tone of voice that Jerry Kelly had used before. And her name is Fanny Wilder.

Jerry Kelly screamed again to be again watching the coming and going of the men and women posted on the mothership. He was silent before asking, with a slight transition in his voice:

"Who told you that?

"One day I spoke to Professor Lehman about you. I know you applied for a position on "Saturn XI" because you were upset with that woman.

"Not true, Marlene. I did it because I wanted to continue my acoustic research and it seemed like an excellent platform. On the other hand ... I was tired of presenting my projects to many sites, without any results! Everywhere they told me I was crazy. As crazy as my father!

Marlene Power also leaned over the railing, losing her gaze at the end of the corridor at her feet as she encouraged:

"I don't think you're crazy, Jerry ... On the contrary!
Thank you, Marlene. You're a good friend!
And the two were silent.

CHAPTER X

On the take-off platform, holding General Peter Masson's hand in his, Walter Lehman insisted:

"Is it essential, Peter?

"It is. Absolutely essential, Walter! And you shouldn't even know.

"Yes ... But we would like to get to Earth, without our names on the passenger list.

"You are not going as passengers. I have included you in the crew of this ship.

"Is the same. I am afraid that, before we arrive, "someone" will know why we are returning and that may cause us some "surprise" ... And unpleasant!

"Stop thinking of a conspiracy, Walter. The Wilder Institute only cared about one thing: all the material you were allowing this young man to use to set up his expensive laboratory. It was when they put the veto. Nothing more!

"I can't help it, Peter. I think like Jerry. One thing is related to another.

"But what you ask of me is not possible. You cannot enter or leave Earth without identifying! Where would we end up? What control could one have like this? And I am responsible for all the personnel that arrive or leave here. I will broadcast your departure and I do not think anything bad will happen to you when you arrive. You will see!

"God hear you, Peter! I wish you the best of luck in your position.

"You know I don't believe in luck, because you know me very well. In this life there are no rewards or punishments that are not a consequence of the results. What logically I call the consequences.

"Anyway, take advice from someone who is older than you and loves you well, Peter. Do not let yourself be ruled by cybernetics too! Never be a machine!

Peter Masson smiled friendly in turn, recommending:

"And you stop being a pure sentimentalist. Now you have those charges on you! If those expensive instruments are nowhere to be found, I am afraid you will have to pay for their cost in some way.

"I have no personal fortune. I never cared about such a trivial thing. If they screw up, I'll pay for it with days in jail.

"Don't be silly! The wise astrophysicist Walter Lehman, who would dare to prosecute him? You will suffer, yes, a serious reprimand. But nothing else! You are one of those who have conquered for everyone immense horizons and great possibilities. You already have to go up, Walter. The schedule is set for ...

"I know! I know! And cold computers don't give a second as a gift. Goodbye, good friend!

"Good luck, Walter!

* * *

In a way it was nice to feel the sensation of returning to the planet where you were born.

The old and worn Earth, tiny in comparison with other planets in the solar system, could not compete even in beauty. Seen from space it was blue: strangely blue, with no possible explanation for laymen.

But endearingly friendly and welcoming.

There, billions of beings lived and toiled, dreaming of one day reaching the distant stars. But this was a collective dream, rather than an individual one. A dream to demonstrate their power, their ingenuity and the capacity of their technology and their science as a race of superior beings, since most of them clung to the spent planet wishing to end their days there.

Why?

The reason was simple: they had been born on Earth, that planet was their first habitation and they felt its attraction.

In the middle of the route, the commander of the spaceship appeared during one of the meals before them and informed them, directly looking at the elderly Walter Lehman:

"I have received a message. We are no longer looking for a shipment of uranium to Alaska. I will have to land in the Sahara, at the World Research Center.

Before giving the astrophysicist time to say something vehemently, Jerry Kelly wanted to know:

"Do you know why this change is due, Commander?

"Since you ask, I will tell you that it is related to the four of you.

He was referring to Walter Lehman, Jerry Kelly, Billy Laughton, and the blonde woman named Marlene Power.

"Let me guess, Commander" asked Jerry. Maybe the order came from the Wilder Institute?

"You got it right! It seems that I must take them there.

With a resigned air, Walter Lehman sighed:

"Goodbye trout! I will no longer be able to fish in Canada.

"We will have to hunt lobsters in the desert," said Billy Laughton.

"Have you been missing from Earth for a long time? "Wanted to know the commander of the ship.

"Pretty. At least I! The old man said.

"Well, they are going to find a lot of changes. Today the bridge that connects San Francisco with Tokyo and another that goes from Chile to Australia is finished. A channel about a hundred kilometers wide crosses Africa from North to South, almost splitting the continent in two. The great desert has ceased to be, becoming a veritable orchard. That is why the World Research Center was installed there. It has an area larger than France: about 600,000 square kilometers, with buildings of about seven hundred floors. There are assigned some two million scientists from all branches of human knowledge, although ...

"I guess again? "Jerry Kelly wanted to play.

"I'll tell you, friend. They are like prisoners!

"I guessed it, Commander!

"It was easy" the astronaut downplayed it. You must have done something very "fat." Once again I had to take some atomic sages there. That is why I know that, although of course it is "assured." Not inside the walls.

"Ah, but is that center surrounded by walls?

"That's right, friend" replied the commander, to the mocking question of Billy Laughton. They all live there, as in a separate nation. Somehow they have to pay for their crimes ... Thankfully they haven't been sent to the channels of Mars! This is hell!

"Do you also know him?

"Yes ... I was born there.

"I should have guessed" Jerry said again.

"Why?

"You have a little greenish skin, my friend. It is characteristic!

The commander of the spaceship went to the door of the cabin, decided to let them continue eating and, already at the door, looking at Jerry Kelly, muttered with some reproach in his voice:

"Very funny! You are very observant.

When they were alone, Marlene Power's right forefinger fluttered in Jerry's face, as if reminding him:

"I told you, Jerry. Nothing good awaits us on Earth!

-And in the « Saturn XI » what awaited us? We did the right thing, Marlene. At least, if upon arrival weinternstill in that World Research Center, we will live. While...

"Jerry is right, boy" intervened Walter Lehman. Besides that I suppose someone will listen to us. We may have committed a crime by using machinery and material improperly. But we have witnessed several crimes!

Billy Laughton looked at the old man who had been his boss on the satellite around the planet Saturn and wanted to check:

"I suppose you will have powerful and influential friends, right, Professor?

"Got them, Billy! And they will listen to me!

"Well: I don't think they'll cut our heads off" the electrodynamic engineer finished reasoning.

"They won't, Billy," Jerry reassured him. I'm sorry I got you into all of this though.

"Silly stuff! "Protested the old man." Your invention will one day be a reality and what happens to us is nothing more than the tribute we have to pay to achieve it. Every scientific advance has cost its own in effort and even sacrifice.

Then he wanted to stop worrying and jovially asked:

"Who is willing to measure his strength with me at chess?

Marlene Power caught the old man's noble intention and agreed:

"Yo, Professor Lehman! And today I will checkmate him! More grim, Billy Laughton grunted, lying on the sofa built into the cabin wall:

"They are going to checkmate us! Look what send us to the desert! Yuck!

CHAPTER XI

The vehicle was flying materially down the wide highway.

It had no wheels. It glided on a layer of air about ten centimeters from the ground, its platform made up of an ionized plastic pneumatic mattress, which allowed the propulsion gases to escape, without the slightest noise in its rapid gliding.

At the astrodrome where they had landed, an escort of twenty soldiers was already waiting for them, dressed in snow-white uniforms and well armed with laser carbines. The one who looked like the boss had gone ahead and as soon as they descended through the hatch he had recited their names, then indicated that they would please get into that vehicle.

It was necessary to obey, although Professor Walter Lehman asked:

"I wish to call Washington, Lieutenant.

"You will do it at the World Research Center, professor. There is no less waiting for you than Mr. Charles Wilder.

They were all amazed, exchanging mute glances between them. Jerry Kelly recalled the warmth, sympathy and friendship that had brought him to the man who was close to being his father-in-law, reassuring his friends:

"I will speak to Mr. Wilder. He was a great friend of my father and he also came to appreciate me very much.

"He may be waiting for you ... with his daughter" commented Marlene Power.

During the journey they did not speak much, absorbed in the panorama that stretched out before them. They could not believe that this was the same region that for centuries and centuries had been the vast Sahara desert.

However, it was true that the miracle of science and technology had turned ten million square kilometers into a veritable orchard, where the predominant color was not the yellow of the burned sand dunes, but the green of lush spring vegetation.

At last they could make out the first buildings of metal, steel and glass and with bold architectural forms, of the World Research Center, raising their domes to the sky on heights that exceeded one kilometer.

"It's fantastic! Billy Laughton exclaimed.

"It is still a gigantic prison," said the woman.

Hearing his comments, the head of the escort said:

"You are wrong, miss. Many of those who live there are happier than those who are free at all.

Those walls surround six hundred thousand square kilometers. It's a whole nation!

Yes, a nation. But of slaves! "Marlene Power remarked.

"There you have everything, miss. The only thing they can't do is get out.

"And by whose order are you detaining us there, Lieutenant? Jerry Kelly wanted to know.

"The order was given to me by my superior. Captain Kraskessy. I do not know any more!

They knew what awaited them and were not surprised to see the speeding vehicle stop at the control of one of the entrance doors. Those men also wore very white uniforms, as did those of their escort.

The procedure was simple, although the twenty men of the escort were left outside and the five detainees were taken over by as many soldiers who led them to a majestic building, which looked like a first-rate hotel.

"I will ask for thesuite room bridal "joked Billy Laughton.

But where they were taken, he went to a room where soon, after the new soldiers were left outside, a dense greenish smoke began to come out from various orifices. The elderly Walter Lehman sat resignedly on the ground, as if willing to let himself die there. Billy Laughton began to run from wall to wall, pounding uselessly on the tightly closed door.

Jerry Kelly searched the thick smoke for Marlene Power's eyes and the two instinctively hugged each other closely.

At least they would die with the pleasant sensation of confessing their love.

* * *

Charles Wilder was a tall man, extremely elegant and neat, who, although he was in his sixties, retained all his vigor.

Jerry Kelly recognized him as soon as he saw him sitting behind the monumental desk, despite the fact that he had not seen the rich and powerful director of the famous Wilder Institute for a long time.

The hand of the man, who was the father of Fanny Wilder, made a gesture inviting:

"Sit down, Jerry. And be welcome!

Before obeying, dull resentful especially at the last anguished sensation he had felt, the young man saluted:

"Thank you, Mr. Wilder. But are you already aware of the "pleasant" reception they have given us?

"Of course, boy. The World Research Center is nothing more than ... How would I put it? ... Yes: a nursery from which our Institute draws. When some new invention, some new research or experiment has good results here, we immediately take over and end up giving it a definitive shape. You know that the Wilder Institute, which my grandfather founded, does not stop scoring good wins!

"We have been treated like criminals, Mr. Wilder!

"In a way you are, dear Jerry.

"How do you say?

"Sit down and I'll explain.

"I want to hear from you, sir.

"You see, Jerry... You have always been as stubborn as your father. He lost his life in those investigations he carried out, and he was a good friend. Maybe my best friend!

"Is that why you always denied me your help?

"Partly yes: I didn't want the same thing to happen to you. But you disappeared with your crazy ideas and your desire to follow what your father started. And you went too far, boy! Nothing less than "Saturn XI", fifteen hundred million kilometers from here!

"I accepted the position, considering that I could continue investigating there.

"And from what I've been told, you did it too!

"So it was, Mr. Wilder. Professor Lehman is an excellent person and he helped me a lot.

"Yes! I already know it! With the funds and material programmed for the Saturn project. It is not like this?

"Mild crime, sir: above all, when I have been about to achieve what can so much benefit Humanity.

The elegant Charles Wilder cocked his head in amusement as he inquired:

"Do you still think that can be of great benefit, Jerry?

"Why not? I have discussed it many times. And I think that if we can make "The voice of the Universe" speak to us, everything will be more ...

He stopped when he saw the gesture of one of those neat and well-groomed hands, hearing its owner say:

"Yes, Jerry. This has already been discussed many times, so we are not going to do it one more time. It is better that I tell you for your government, that when I learned from the Governing Board of the Institute of everything that happened, although I have not been able to get you to be freed from all responsibility, I have managed to receive special treatment.

"And my friends?

Charles Wilder seemed to hesitate before commenting:

"Well ... They'll be fine here. Don't you know this is like a great nation It already has more than two million inhabitants!

"You mean two million prisoners, Mr. Wilder

"Why call them that, when they can roam freely within this immense enclosure? The World Research Center is bigger than Spain. Everything here is modern, clean, made of glass and steel, Jerry. Transparent plastic buildings resist fire, forming high mountains of huge blocks. Rotating platforms making houses and windows follow the path of the sun. Moving streets with endless belts, on which you can go from one place to another without getting tired. Silent elevators that will take you up to more than a thousand meters high, or that will descend into the bowels of the earth, vomiting thousands of workers into the most secret laboratories. Don't you know that here we are rehearsing new life forms?

"Perhaps the way for man to live a slave, while willingly accepting that condition, Mr. Wilder?

The powerful financier and industrialist smiled, brushing his neat little mustache as he celebrated:

"You're still the same, Jerry! You have not changed!

Now that I think about it, Mr. Wilder, I have the feeling that you have changed.

He deliberately paused before adding to the soon:

"Or maybe it was always like that and I didn't realize it.

"Jerry, boy. We will not advance with hurtful comments.

"Let's drop it then and get down to business, Mr. Wilder. Why does it bother you so much that I get what I set out to do?

"Bother me? No, son, no! On the contrary!

"Well, let me tell you that you have a vague and annoying feeling that it was you ... you who prevented it!

Charles Wilder jumped to his feet, protesting:

"Are you accusing me of something, boy?

"I cannot do it in a specific way. I'm missing data, but ...

"You will have to rectify, Jerry. I have found out everything, because it is natural that this is the case. I am the managing director of the Wilder Institute after all!

"That is precisely why I am surprised not to have more support from you.

"You have my support, boy. But I have not written

laws or statutes. What was stolen by you is worth many millions ... And that is why they have brought you here!

"Without trial, sir? No sentence? Have the laws and the sense of justice changed so much, since we left the Earth? Or is it that all of it has already become a gigantic World Research Center, in which only the powerful like you rule, the privileged few who can live as they please, marching where they please?

"I said, Jerry. You are against me!

"How could we not be, when they have brought us two escorts here, they have watched us, they have put us in a room spraying us with smoke, with the anguish of thinking that they gassed us there?

"But man! They are common measurements. Disinfection must be done everywhere.

"Be warned, Mr. Wilder!

Come on, come on, boy! It's not important.

"He does! Especially when you don't want to treat human beings as if they were machines. Yes: I have already seen that as you say here everything is neat, everything clean, everything ultramodern. And of course, all rationalized, subjected to the omnipotence of those who govern this gigantic prison, who will even delegate their functions to the electronic brains, which will be the ones who will really give the orders ...

Jerry Kelly had gotten excited and went on:

"Yes, Mr. Wilder: I have been able to see that everything is in its place and everything is in order. Every minute controlled. Each action, previously programmed. I bet that nothing is improvised here either on the fly and the human beings who live here, like the machines, will never make a decision that has not been approved by the computer before ... Figures, numbers, figures and in the end the Outcome. Without protest! Without modifying anything on your own! Completely annulled the personality of higher beings, passing beings! It is not like this?

Charles Wilder had ended up crossing his careful hands, watching him between smiling and amused, his intelligent and extremely astute eyes shining.

"Well, I don't like all of that! "The young man before him ended up shouting." And if it is true that he appreciates me in something, that my father was his best friend ...

"Don't go on, Jerry... My power isn't that high. I can't get you out of here!

"At least they will set a deadline for us. They can't keep us here forever. We have not committed any crime!

Gently flipping through some papers before him, Charles Wilder whispered quietly, as if speaking to himself, but loud enough to be heard.

"So, above all ... I have learned that in all your unfortunate business there were quite a few deaths, right, Jerry?

Jerry Kelly jumped up:

"Please, Mr. Wilder! Don't confuse things. These deaths occurred precisely when they tried to eliminate us, in view of the fact that the high explosive that was placed in our spacecraft, was discovered and disassembled.

"Okay, Jerry! Okay ... I already told you that I read the report briefly. If you say so, boy ...

"There is more, sir. Are they not going to investigate this Gassman, this Louis Streisand and why did they act like that? We were sent on a suicide mission!

"Men...! As much as that, Jerry! I don't know ... Fortunately, I see you here, healthy and strong, and with the same energy as always. Why this excitement?

"I have told you, sir. Injustices revolt me!

"It is not entirely the case to send you here. Think and nobly accept some responsibility. And above all, trust that, because of what you meant to my daughter and what your father was to me, I will soon fix this whole mess. Including your friends, ea! He exclaimed at the end, as if conceding.

Jerry Kelly had calmed down, becoming interested when he heard him quote the woman he had once loved so much:

"How is Fanny, ..?

"Well well! You know that she was never lacking for anything, she travels, she goes on cruises, she has many friends ... and she spends her life in the most expensive couturiers in the world!

"That's a good sign, Mr. Wilder. They are the will to live.

"Of course! It's been a long time since he overcame the crisis, when he broke up with you ...

"I'm glad.

Charles Wilder got up rubbing his hands, ending the interview at the conclusion:

"Well, Jerry: we agreed that when a few weeks pass I will look to fix everything. For the moment they will set you up well and your stay here will not be so unpleasant, as long as you abide by the rules. You will see that they are not rigorous at all!

"I will appreciate everything you do for me and my friends, Mr. Wilder.

"It doesn't matter, man. Although, yes, boy. You will have to work, dedicate yourself to something! You are all scientists and your brains are worth a lot. What would you like to spend your time on?

"You know that, sir. On acoustics!

Charles Wilder seemed to frown, but instantly agreed:

"You'll find out what you like, Jerry! And let's see if it's true that one day you will make us all hear "The voice of the Universe"!

"I'll get it, Mr. Wilder. I just need the necessary means, just as I had already achieved on "Saturn XI."

"I'll have them provide you with those means, boy. This World Research Center is created for that. No idea should be wasted! No brain should let its fruit go to waste! You will see!

They went out together and when they separated the powerful and elegant Charles Wilder still promised:

"The Wilder Institute will be the first to launch your invention!

CHAPTER XII

Charles Wilder showed signs of keeping his word.

Jerry Kelly was assigned to a workshop where, outside of the controlled hours for other tasks, he and his friends could investigate what had been interrupted on the "Saturn XI", so many hundreds of thousands of kilometers away, in full heart of what had been the arid Sahara desert.

Only, for one reason or another, he did not get the material he needed.

So the months went by, forcibly having to acclimate to the discipline of the World Research Center, where other scientists also arrested were advancing much more than he in their research.

The mighty Charles Wilder was frequently there, but he did not always deign to welcome the man who had long been his daughter's fiancé. He only did it a couple of times, and the last time he had said reluctantly:

"Sorry, Jerry. I have a lot of work. I promise you that I will take care of your matter.

"Mr. Wilder... I know you won't!

"What nonsense, boy! What happens is that I have too many things in my head and I cannot attend to everything. Every time I visit this center, I have to take a good pile of files to see if any of the findings can be useful to the Wilder Institute.

He pointed to the private secretary who always accompanied him, indicating:

Take note, Makensy. We need to take care of Jerry. And now, if you'll allow me, boy ...

"Of course, Mr. Wilder. You have a lot to do and the permission they gave me ends in a few minutes. I won't bother you anymore!

"It is no hassle. They told me that you are making progress little by little and that you have managed to build new devices that ...

"They are not very powerful, sir. That way I will never end. I need ultra-sensitive antennas, good tape recorders, proper filters, and a host of other things!

"What's happening? They don't supply everything you ask for?

"They never do! When one thing is not lacking, it is another. But it's the same to me!

From the door, before saying goodbye, he announced:

"We are getting acclimatized, Mr. Wilder. Do not worry! I think one of these days Marlene and I will get married and stay here forever.

"I already told you it wasn't that bad, though… Of course I'll get you out!

Charles Wilder absently flipped through documents without seeing that Jerry Kelly had left the office. When he raised his head and looked at his private secretary, a lifelong friend of his, he inquired:

"Has that fool gone yet, Makensy?

"Yes, Charles. Why don't you finish this comedy at once?

"For what? Deep down it amuses me. It is always convenient to pass as a good person and the authorities, The center likes to see me worried about one of the internees.

"Perhaps they would like to know that you wanted to get rid of him, as you did with his father.

Charles Wilder gave a nervous start and chided:

"Do you want to shut up? I don't like to talk about it. I had to kill Jerry's father because he was insolent with me, with the fact that we were friends he did not respect me and did whatever he wanted in the Institute that my grandfather founded. He was obsessed with his acoustic laws and I didn't like those investigations.

"Take! To anybody! If he succeeds, he might "hunt down" the sound waves of many of your conversations and … Goodbye to the great and powerful Charles Wilder!

"You can't speak either, Makensy. You also have a lot to hide!

"Less than you, Charles. You got higher!

"Are we going to throw our dirty laundry in our faces now?

"No, Charles. But I don't like that, on top of that, you make fun of that boy.

"What do you want me to do? I got him to be included with his friends in the expedition to the rings of Saturn, after receiving the information from Gassman. That boy is very smart and went further than his father. He went to "Saturn XI" and that old idiot Walter Lehman gave him everything that I had always denied him. He built his diabolical devices and would have made his invention a reality. He had spoken to me many times about him and I tell you that such a thing can be achieved. They are fixed laws of acoustics, Makensy! Immutable laws!

"Is that why you tried to eliminate him too?

"And to all his collaborators! For men like you and me, the world is fine like this. No fault makes us that our words may one day be "hunted as if they were butterflies and those who should not hear them again. Don't you think?

"Yes, but you saw that they were saved.

"Because of the greed of stupid Luis Streisand. I wanted to keep the instruments and packed others, leading to the deception being discovered.

"Didn't you also place an atomic device on the ship?

"Yes, but I tell you they found out and came back. Then, back on the mothership, what could I do? It was not convenient to raise more suspicions: General Peter Masson rules there and he is a very upright person.

Charles Wilder paced the spacious office, well-groomed hands clasped behind his back, before glancing at his assistant and continuing:

"Here they are good. If we don't file charges at the Wilder Institute. They will never get out of here! They can't bother me.

Silence reigned between the two before Makensy said:

"Charles ... Wouldn't it be better to cause another 'accident'? If the father was burned to death, as everyone believes, when he was researching his invention, the same could happen to the son, don't you think?

"I'm going to tell you something, Makensy... You don't have to hate Jerry Kelly so much. One day or another my daughter will stop thinking about him, and you can marry her. Why complicate us more?

"And I will speak to you frankly, Charles. I'm getting tired of waiting! Fanny still loves that genius ... And Jerry Kelly may one day get out of here!

"Do not believe it.

"What about the authorities at that center? From time to time there are reviews of the causes and the crime of these men is not so much. With a couple of years ...

"I am telling you no! I'll take care of that. That boy you just heard that he will end up marrying the girl who came with them. Here they can live happily and forget about everything. Many do!

"Men like Jerry never fit into this life. It would be better to finish with him! What if one day he gets all the material he needs? Can you imagine the one who would form "hunting" as he says all the words that float in space?

"They never give him the precise material. I have ordered it!

What if he succeeds?

"It's okay! Do what you want, Makensy. It's up to you!

"Thank you, Charles... But I want Fanny to know that she died somewhere! You must understand me.

"Accepted friend. But do the best you can. I don't want trouble!

"Don't worry ... I already have experience in causing" fortuitous accidents. "

* * *

The experience that Makensy had bragged about to his boss and friend this time was of no use to him.

That same afternoon he and Charles Wilder were arrested by the same authorities at the World Research Center, where the two of them were among the people who had bossed around the most up to that day.

But they were arrested before irrefutable evidence.

"The voice of the Universe" had spoken!

Jerry Kelly was able to present a tape of the conversation that the two men had had in his monumental office on the three hundred and fourteenth floor and more than three miles from the experimental workshop of the acoustic engineer ... who had managed to "hunt down" that one! conversation with a rudimentary team built by himself, despite the refusal of certain items of the material he needed!

"I made up for the lack of means with ingenuity" clarified Jerry Kelly.

"But then ... your invention is a fact?

"It will be when it is more sophisticated and can be used to 'hunt down' sound waves that have continued to spread out in space for centuries. In this case I was able to do it because I had all the most accurate data. Place where I had left Mr. Wilder, exact time, situation, ambient temperature and some other things that it was easy for me to calculate.

He took them into his rudimentary workshop, showing them his instruments by expanding:

"The distance was short and these simple antennas were able to pick up the sound vibrations coming out of that building. The filters were selecting all the noises, nuancing them and eliminating those that did not interest me ... The rest was simple!

"Did you suspect Mr. Wilder?

Jerry Kelly was sincere in saying:

"I never thought he had murdered my father, but I did suspect that, for some reason, he did not want my investigations to be successful.

From there to relate to everything that happened on "Saturn XI", there was a step that I finally took when I observed that he still did not fulfill his promises ...

"He is a very influential man, but before this test ... They have no possible defense! What you have achieved is simply wonderful. Nothing less than to take back everything that men talk about!

"Not everything that they speak, but what past generations have spoken.

"Really fantastic!

"True ... But very delicate!

"Exactly!

"However, it is worth continuing to fight to achieve it in a total way. Think that, just as Charles Wilder and that scoundrel Makensy will receive their punishment, the same awaits all the guilty as all the secret criminal conspiracies can be discovered.

"Then there will be no secrets, because the Universe will speak!

* * *

What Charles Wilder did get right was when he said that the Institute his grandfather had founded would finance the research and assembly costs of what everyone now called Jerry Kelly's "invention."

It is true that there was still a lot of work to be done, but the following tests that he carried out ensured success.

An artificial satellite was sent around the last planet in the solar system, so that while it was in orbit around Pluto it would serve as an ideal platform from which the strange acoustic instruments could begin to "hunt" the sounds.

And the new satellite was called "The voice of the Universe."

Jerry Kelly was appointed in charge of that new

ingenuity of the man, while Dr. Marlene Power became his wife and his most faithful collaborator.

And there, in the confines of the solar system, looking into the hyperspace that they would have to probe to make their dreams come true, they could savor the truth of their love that so many difficult trials had managed to save.

They were in love with the truth.

The absolute truth that one day they could offer as a dangerous gift to the whole world ...

The only thing that remained to be known was whether man would withstand the difficult test when "The voice of the Universe" began to speak ...

END